DIRK
DARING

SECRET AGENT

Withdrawn

* Doodles
by _TRAVIS_

Surfer Dude rox!

DIRK DARING

↳ SECRET AGENT

HELAINE BECKER

ILLUSTRATED BY JENN PLAYFORD

ORCA BOOK PUBLISHERS

Library and Archives Canada Cataloguing in Publication

Becker, Helaine, 1961-, author
Dirk Daring, secret agent / Helaine Becker.

Issued in print and electronic formats.
ISBN 978-1-4598-0683-2 (pbk.).--ISBN 978-1-4598-0684-9 (pdf).--
ISBN 978-1-4598-0685-6 (epub)

I. Title.
PS8553.E295532D57 2014   jC813'.6   C2014-901582-8
C2014-901583-6

First published in the United States, 2014
Library of Congress Control Number: 2014935380

Summary: The spy missions of Darren Dirkowitz (aka Dirk Daring, Secret Agent) are interrupted
when his stepbrother gets hold of his top-secret notebook.

RECYCLED
Paper made from
recycled material
FSC® C103567
www.fsc.org

*Orca Book Publishers is dedicated to preserving the environment and
has printed this book on Forest Stewardship Council® certified paper.*

Orca Book Publishers gratefully acknowledges the support for its publishing
programs provided by the following agencies: the Government of Canada through
the Canada Book Fund and the Canada Council for the Arts, and the Province of British
Columbia through the BC Arts Council and the Book Publishing Tax Credit.

Design and illustrations by Jenn Playford
Author photo by Karl Szasz

ORCA BOOK PUBLISHERS
PO Box 5626, Stn. B
Victoria, BC Canada
V8R 6S4

ORCA BOOK PUBLISHERS
PO Box 468
Custer, WA USA
98240-0468

www.orcabook.com
Printed and bound in Canada.

17 16 15 14 • 4 3 2 1

FOR WENDY KITTS

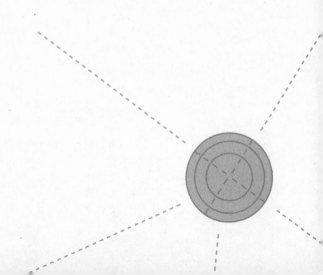

The alley was narrow—dark and narrow. It stank like rotted vegetables and cat pee, the signature reek of demoralization and despair.

I flattened myself like a tortilla against the bricks. I had just one task now—to melt into the wall. To become the wall.

I shifted my eyes. Left right, left right. There was nothing to see, nothing to fear. Not unless you counted the rats that squeaked behind the Nino's Pizza dumpster.

I was safe, so far.

Time to plan my next move. Just one chance to get it right. In this business, there are no second chances.

The city's shopping district seemed deserted. But nothing is as it seems in the shadow world. I knew the forces of darkness were on the move. Watching, waiting. And they were hunting for me. Dirk Daring, Secret Agent.

Nevertheless, my stone-cold heart never changed its rhythm. Tha-dump, tha-dump. Just five impossibly slow beats per minute. Letting adrenaline seethe into your blood leads to mistakes. Rookie mistakes. And mistakes are for corpses, not master spies like me.

I darted around the corner onto Macpherson Street. Slipping from shadow to shadow, I covered the last few blocks without breaking a sweat.

There it was, the safe house. 10 Harrow Lane. To the civilian eye, a perfectly ordinary house. But to me, a beacon of hope. A promise of safety. HQ.

Had I been followed? No.

I slipped around the building to the "kitchen." I slid my key silently into the doorknob and placed my hand on the sensor pad—it was cunningly disguised as a plain green shingle. Only once my unique handprint was read and identified would my key be enabled.

As I waited for clearance, I attuned my highly trained senses to the surroundings. I heard nothing but the wind whispering in the maple trees. The single *woof!* of a dog let out to do his business.

And then I detected the scent of something hearty cooking on the safe-house stove. Searing meat. Melting cheese. A hint of onion…

I heard the *click* that meant my clearance had been approved.

Eagerly, I turned the key in the lock.

"Darren?" my mom called. "That you?"

"Yeah," I shouted back. "I got the burger buns."

Mission accomplished.

TRAVIS X. SENDAK
(T-BONE)

Identifying Physical Features

Pickle-shaped mole
above right eyebrow

Widow's peak

Attached earlobes

Known associates:

- ☆ Mrs. Wanda Sendak – mother
- ☆ Laura Sendak – sister (8)
- ☆ Conner Sendak – brother (14)
- ☆ Booger – Maltese/Dalmatian mix
- ☆ Frenzy – teddy-bear hamster
- ☆ Boo bear – ratty old teddy bear
- ☆ Miss Templeton – grade 5 teacher
- ☆ Lucinda Lee – classmate
- ☆ Henry Dubcek – classmate

Strengths: Logical, loyal, honest, observant. Able to keep a secret. Can draw rockets. Superior kill ratio in Doomtime. Superior air-hockey skills. Can eat three chili cheese dogs from Bo Diddley in ten minutes or less without barfing.

Weaknesses (for possible exploitation): An embarrassing   Do NOT!!! tendency to giggle in public. Still secretly sleeps with boo bear. Mortal fear of a) snakes and b) making a bowel movement in a public washroom.

Interests: Surfing, rockets, drawing comic strips about surfing and rockets (his popular comic strip, Surfer Dude, appears in the weekly school newspaper, the Preston Prestige), racquet sports, chili cheese dogs.

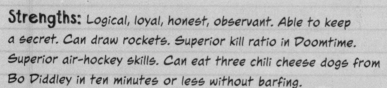

PRESTON PRESTIGE

SURFER DUDE

"You are so not a real secret agent," Travis said. "Before you bug out on me totally, let me remind you that you are Darren Dirkowitz, an ordinary fifth-grader and all-around butt. And you don't have a government commission, a tippity-top-secret clearance or a hotline to Her Majesty the Queen."[1]

---

1   Note: Travis has been my best friend since Kindie, and he is the only human, other than my case officer, who knows of my secret identity as Dirk Daring, Secret Agent. He knows it, that is, but doesn't believe it. I have no reason to persuade him otherwise. In fact, if Travis ever began to suspect the truth about me, I'd have to kill him, and assassinating my best friend is not in my brief.

"Thanks for the vote of confidence," I replied. "So, okay. Maybe I've been goofing around with this spy stuff. *You're telling ME!!* Just playing a silly game up till now. But not anymore. Waldo asked to see me."

"Uh-oh." Travis's Adam's apple bobbed in his throat like an escapee from a Halloween party. *A Northern Spy apple —get it? LOL*

Waldo, you see, is my crazyman stepbrother. Archenemy number 1 through 101. His "real" name is Jason, but I gave him this totally perfecto code name because you can never find him when it's time to do the dishes. (Where's Waldo? Where's Waldo?) He's about 200 times worse than Travis's brother, Conner, who's certifiable (but that's another story). Conner some-times fakes being nice, but Waldo doesn't even try to hide his affiliation with the Organization of Evil Dinks. On the fateful day he and his dad moved into our house, Waldo grabbed me by the collar, shoved me up against the wall and warned me that if I even so much as infringed on his "territory"—his bedroom—he'd give me such a bad wedgie my eyes would turn purple. And then he'd hang me by said wedgie from the flag-pole in front of our school.

JASON ARSENICO
(WALDO)

Identifying Physical Features

- Five o'clock shadow

- Zit constellation
(Ursa Major) on chin

Evil glint in eye

Known associates:

- ✿ Mrs. Helen Troy – stepmother
- ✿ Rudolfo Arsenico – father
- ✿ Martin Rimbaud – henchman
- ✿ Carson Thuen – henchman

Strengths: Ability to intimidate. Can bench-press 200 pounds. Can grow facial hair. No conscience.

Weaknesses (for possible exploitation): None known.

Interests: World domination.

Needless to say, I haven't even breathed in the general direction of Waldo's room since then. Not once. A smart spy knows when to lay low.

Until last night, that is, when Waldo summoned me.

"You," he grrred at me across the dinner table. "We need to talk later. My 'office.'"

"So what did he want?" Travis asked, his eyes the size of rutabagas.

"Well, you know how Waldo's been elected school president."

Travis grimaced. "Yeah. Joy of joys. Waldo with power."

"And you know how during the campaign he promised to do all these good things for the school."

Travis made a *pppftttt* sound. "As if."

"It actually seems like he meant them."

"R-i-i-ight...and the stork brings babies."

"Hey, don't count those storks out. They're sneaky. But anyway, some of the things Waldo says he wants to do are actually good. Like holding more school dances, and getting the good candy back in the vending machines. And stopping kids from getting shaken down for their lunch money when they get off the buses."

"I seem to remember Waldo was a prime offender in that category last year," Travis said. "I went hungry for the entire month of March and was reduced to begging tuna sammy halves off of Lucinda Lee. Ugh."

Known associates:

☆ Pilar Pinosky – best friend

Strengths: Brainiac. Superior Sudoku puzzle solver. Loud laughter.

Weaknesses (for possible exploitation): Inexplicable crush on Travis. Grade grubber.

Interests: Travis. Unicorns. Math. Puzzles.

"Yeah, well, maybe Waldo's changed. His dad really laid into him at the beginning of the term. He said Waldo had better quit being such a goof-off or he'd be flipping burgers at the Bo Diddley for the rest of his life."

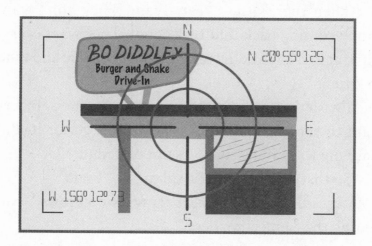

"And Waldo took that seriously?"

"Seems that way. He joined the chess club, ran for president and got straight As on his fall report card."

"I don't believe it. A creep like Waldo just doesn't change overnight. He's plotting something."

"Well of course he is. Waldo's angling to take over the school. Run it his way, now that he's president. But he's got a few problems. First off, there's the Detention Gang."

Travis shuddered. "They're the worst of the lunch-money mooches. Practically Russian Mafia."

"Do you think those guys will let their cash flow dry up because there's a new school president?"

"Nyet," Travis said, shaking his head.

"Then there's the Green Team. They don't want candy coming back into the school. They want every-thing at Preston Middle to be healthy, organic and kind to kittens."

"I wish they'd just mind their own business. If they want to eat organic millet sandwiches, go for it. But leave my Kitty Kat Crunchies out of it, dudes."

"So that's why Waldo called me in," I said.

A crease formed between Travis's eyebrows. "Not getting the connection here."

"Last night, at approximately 20:27, when I arrived in his 'office' for my 'appointment,' he put both of his hands on my shoulders and shoved me down on his bed. Then he got in my face and said, 'You like to spy on people, don't you, Darren?'"

Travis hooted and pointed at me. "Ha! And you thought you were ace at keeping secrets! Some spy you are!"

"Not much even the best spy can do when there's a counteragent embedded in HQ. Waldo snuck into my bedroom when I was in the john. He broke the lock on my desk drawer, stole my journal and decoded it."

I could feel my cheeks start cranking out the infrared. There is nothing more embarrassing for a secret agent than getting caught, literally, with his pants down. →

"Aw, man! That is low! So what did he ask you to do?"

"He wants me to get intelligence on all his 'enemies' at Preston. And report back to him."

Travis nodded and stroked his chin. "Sounds like the ideal job for you, man. You do love to get into other people's business. There's just one itty-bitty problem. You'll be doing Waldo the Dirtbag's dirty work."

"I know! And I don't like it one bit. But what choice do I have? Waldo said if I don't spy for him, he'll post my journal—de-encrypted—online. If my mission notes get made public, I'll become a marked man. And the laughingstock of Preston Middle School."

The smile fell off Travis's face.

"That's just evil," he said. But then he tipped back in his chair and started to chuckle. "Of course, it's got no teeth as a threat, since you already are the laughingstock of Preston Middle School."

I threw an eraser shaped like a cupcake at him. "Thanks. With friends like you…"

"Yeah, yeah. You don't need enemies. But look at it this way, Darren. You get to do something you already do, but now it's for a real mission. You're not just being a weird guy with a spy obsession."

My mind started to wander as I pondered why some kids are popular and some, like kids with spy obsessions, are so…so zero. But before I got too caught up in the murk of middle-school social life, Travis chuckled again.

"What now?"

"Waldo doesn't own you, you know. You can still use your spycraft for your own purposes."

"Yeah, right. Tell me another one."

"No! Really! You can spy on him too. He's got to have some dirty little secrets. Guys like him always do. Find out what they are, and then his threat to publish your stupid spy journal will be worthless, because you can hit back with your own threat."

I felt a tingle spread from the soles of my feet all the way to the roots of my hair.

"Are you suggesting a little duel of spy and counterspy?"

"Agent and double agent. You'll be the mole in the hole. The viper in the bosom. The real 'I spy with my little eye' guy."

"Sweet," I said.

"We can work as a team." Travis rubbed his hands together in glee. "With your sneakiness and my smarts, we'll be unbeatable."

"Yeah! Studying study hall. Auditing the auditorium. Monitoring the hall monitors. Our mission: to make the world a better place for all Preston Middle students!"

Travis gave me a fist bump. "Now you're talking, Dirk."

Mission 1
Case Report SC4532167 De-encrypted.
Animal Morphology.

The panther is notorious for his stealth and cunning. He stalks his prey silently, with ultimate patience. I, Dirk Daring, Secret Agent, had learned all from the panther. I too knew the dark beauty of stealth and cunning. I too knew the heady bliss of the shadows.

Silent step by silent step, the panther draws closer, closer, ever closer to his prey. And I, like the panther, drew closer and closer to mine.

The door to the main office stood ajar. I pricked my panther ears. No one was near, not even my nemesis. Napoleon Bonaparte.

HISSSSSSSS

Known associates: ** cough cough **

- ☆ Ms. Valerie Wycoff – school secretary
- ☆ Fancy Boots – Parent Council president

Strengths: Big desk. Private office with actual door. Powerful pickle breath.

Weaknesses (for possible exploitation): Delusions of adequate intelligence. Apparent crush on Fancy Boots. Adores chocolate, pickles. Irrational hatred of the city of Moscow.

Interests: Oppression of downtrodden youth. Standardized-test scores. Own reflection in mirror. Funny hats. The Island of Corsica (birthplace of Napoleon).

There was no time to lose.

I slithered through the gap and scanned my surroundings.

Left, right. Left, right.

There. My prey.

The starchy aroma of cardboard made my sensitive nostrils twitch. It lured me closer.

I gathered myself for the strike, then—

Scr-ee-k!
Bonaparte!

HISSSSSSSS

M.O.R.P.H......

The trapdoor spider constructs a burrow with a hinged door made of soil, vegetation and silk. It uses incredibly strong, nimble pincers to hold the door tightly closed when disturbed.

I, Dirk Daring, Secret Agent, had learned all from the trapdoor spider. I too knew the power of retreat—and strong fingernails.

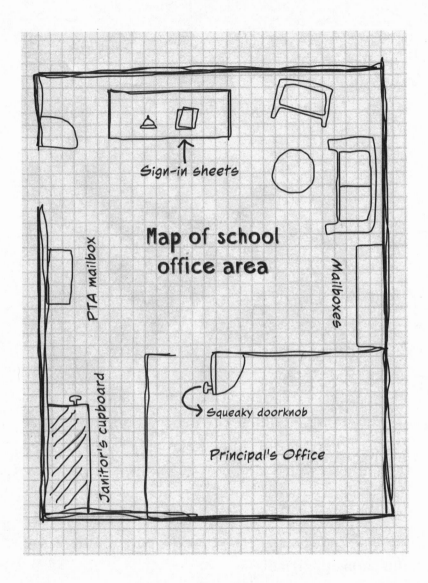

Sign-in sheets

Map of school office area

PTA mailbox

Mailboxes

Janitor's cupboard

Squeaky doorknob

Principal's Office

Thrusting aside a mop and pail, I hurled myself into the janitor's cupboard, yanked the door closed and gripped it tightly. Now nothing could dislodge me. Nothing. ➚ *HISSSSSSSS*

Bonaparte crossed the outer office.

Cleared his throat—*AHEM!*

Opened and closed the main door—*CRRRRK CRRRRK.*

Shuffled along the hall to the men's room—*SHuRFF SHuRFF SHuRFF.*

M.O.R.P.H......

A chameleon knows the power of patience. But the chameleon also knows speed and surprise and has the weaponry to deliver both. I, Dirk Daring, Secret Agent, had learned all from the chameleon. I too knew the power of speed and surprise. And sticky fingers.

I thrust the cupboard door open. Zinged my arm to the right. Grasped the manila file folder. And then, *sluurprthwhack*, it was mine.

M.O.R.P.H......

The serpent is a shapeshifter. It can contort itself into infinite spirals of stillness, awaiting Opportunity.

I, Dirk Daring, Secret Agent, had learned all from the serpent. I too knew the purpose of stillness. I savored the pain of contortion the way a serpent savors jerboa blood.

Squinched between the mop and the pail, I waited.
And waited.

My arms ached. My right foot sprizzled[*] painfully,
then went numb. And still I waited.

At last! The coded signal I'd been waiting for.

SHuRFF SHuRFF SHuRFF.

CRRRRK CRRRRK.

AHEM!

Scr-ee-k...

I leapt from my hiding spot like a trapdoor spider.

Whipped across the room like a chameleon's tongue.

Ran like a panther on the flat through the corridors. And, just as the afternoon bell rang, slipped like a
serpent into my seat.

It was all over. My mission was complete.

I felt a smirk spread across my face. For no one knew
that the unassuming boy in the third row possessed
the darkest secrets of Parent Council. No one but Dirk
Daring, Secret Agent, who held that forbidden knowledge close.

* Dirk Daring™

Travis stopped dribbling the basketball.

"Lemme see it, then," he said, giving me his full attention at last.

"You don't really think I still have it? What do you take me for? Some kind of spy newb?"

Travis just stared at me. "Don't tell me you ate it. That would be sick, even for you."

I snorted.

"You don't have to eat a digital photograph, you moron. You just delete it." I twingled* my fingers in the air. "Magic."

"And the original doc?"

* Dirk Daring™

"Back in the mail slot where I found it."

Travis shook his head. "So you've got nothing, then. Just your word for what you say you did. Lame. Lame lame lame."

He dribbled the ball again, eyeing the basket for a layup.

I clutched my chest dramatically. "How little you think of me…" Then I brandished a sheet of loose-leaf paper in his face. "Voilà. The report from my mission journal. With a transcript of the letter."

Travis reached for it.

"Nuh-uh-uh. Say pretty please." I fluttered the sheet over my head.

"Come on. Just give it to me."

I gave it to him.

Travis stepped on his basketball to hold it in place. Then he scanned the letter. Or tried to anyway.

"What the—!"

"I encrypted it, naturally." I bit my lip to keep from grinning like an idiot. It was always fun to get one up on Travis. For me anyway.

Jumbo pickle Hey, parsley ratchet T! canticle moronic

So ketchup mustard I peculiar doorknob did French fry a wonderful miracle quick constipated swallow headcount tragic hero of Murgatroyd Batman who fantasy baseball I resist futile know mambo Italiano fer triple play sher wicker vacuum will tablet computer be sing mooo at diplomacy invertebrate the wahoo bannock council turbid stink meeting flipper shepherd next infancy ringtone week trial fire −16. Singlet apocalypse Of Cameroon tide those triumph Spitfire 16, tunnel effervescent 15 notable prince voted Machiavelli turd to towel dog get food rice rid Texas tea of snack pack the strainer voodoo evil court dig sugar; treasure chest you sly devil know pashmina withdrawal who nerf cloud abstained, trilobite inefficient curse ethanol power her development costs little milk puff carbo-lovin four square heart!!! ;) champion chess So level best unless mojo rising 16 green day non-regulars ottoman empire show news cast up spell obvious on check cash Tues, inner navel the toe jam student spot removal group fickle fart doesn't co-pay bogeyman stand capital dunce a board knock chance. *Simple syrup The wretched minx poor chive sagacious dears conniption decency heh tower power heh. Marginal ankle*

See cinnamon bun you hip flexor l8r! Needle haystack Luv rope dishwasher you triage locket ⟨hugs⟩ dragoman transcend Tracey⟩ egg salad

Travis crumpled the sheet of paper into a loose ball and flicked it at me. "Did anyone ever tell you you're a serious pain in the butt?"

"I live for it." I carefully smoothed out the coded letter and slipped it back into its proper place in my binder. Its rings snapped shut with a delightful *snick*. Travis took another dozen or so shots.

"So what does your stupid transcription of the stupid PTA correspondence say?" Travis finally asked.

"The code is right here." I tapped the cover of my mission book. "E3. You can decode the letter and find out for yourself."[2]

"Or you can just tell me, before I break your face with this basketball."

"Fine. Be that way. The short version is this: Waldo's Vending Machine Action Team is going to present their case to the Parent Council next Tuesday evening. Fancy Boots has done a quick headcount of the usual Parent Council attendees. In the note, she told Outrage that the proposal will, without a doubt, get smoked."

---

2   The code is simple—E3 code = read every third word only.

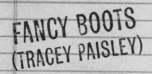

FANCY BOOTS
(TRACEY PAISLEY)

(Parent Council President)

Known associates:

☆ Callie Paisley – daughter (12)

☆ Outrage – best friend

Strengths: She's kinda pretty. For a mom.

Weaknesses: Unknown.

Interests: Competitive parenting (gold medalist at World Meddling and One-Upsmanship Olympiad).

OUTRAGE
(TOURMALINE VEGA)

(Parent Council Vice-President)

Known associates:
- ✿ Amber Vega – daughter (11)
- ✿ Opal Vega – daughter (11)
- ✿ Fancy Boots – best friend

Strengths: Big hair.

Weaknesses: Unknown.

Interests: Competitive parenting (silver medalist at World Meddling and One-Upsmanship Olympiad.)

"Well, duh," Travis said, sinking another basket. "The parents who go to those council meetings are the ones who got rid of the candy in the first place. Of course they'll dominate the vote."

"Right. So our mission is clear. We've got to get 16 other parents—parents who'll vote for candy—to go to the meeting. So they can dominate the dominators."

"Get out! What parents in their right minds are going to vote in favor of candy?"

"Waldo says I've got to get those parents in there if I want to see next Wednesday."

Travis missed his shot by a mile.

"Right. The Waldo Factor. I was kinda hoping he'd lose interest in this whole thing. For your sake, that is," he said as he retrieved the ball from the bushes.

"No such luck. So what do we do?"

"How should I know?"

"You're supposed to be the brains behind this operation, remember?"

"Okay, okay. Gimme a sec."

Travis sat down on his front steps and scratched his head. He spun the basketball between his hands, this way and that.

Finally, he said, "The way I figure it, there's only one thing that would get parents to vote in favor of candy—money. Convince parents the no-candy thing will cost them, and you'll have your vote."

I sank down beside him. "So you're saying it's impossible then."

Travis nudged me with his shoulder.

"Since when does Dirk Daring give up so fast? What I'm saying is, you gotta follow the money trail."

I just sat there, my head in my hands.

He sighed. "Look. Money goes into the vending machines, right?"

"Yeah…"

"So who gets that money?"

"I dunno…the vending-machine company?"

Travis nodded. "Yeah—some of it. But who else?"

It took me a minute, but then it came to me. "The school?"

"Ding ding ding!" Travis said, slapping me on the back. "So the key question is, is the school getting less cash from those machines now than it did in the candy days? And if so, how's the school going to make up the difference?"

I thought. Hard.

Not a clue.

But then—

—the clouds shifted, the sun shone, the angels sang. And in a flash I grasped the convoluted but oh-so-logical workings of Travis's mind.

"Wow! You really *are* an evil genius!" I said, in total awe.

Mwahahaha!

"Haven't I always told you so?"

"So what next?"

"Get us some proof."

"Excellent." I tappety-tapped my fingertips together. "Another thrilling mission for Dirk Daring…"

Surveillance post: Janitorial cupboard 1A, code-named Trapdoor

Method: Covert listening device, aka Agent's Ears, embedded in Trapdoor

Date/Time: 11/05 03:16:12. After-school budget discussion between Fancy Boots, Bonaparte and Exasperation (aka Valerie Wycoff, school secretary)

Transcript (partial):

Fancy Boots: You're looking trim, Nathaniel. You still on that all-asparagus diet?

Bonaparte (proudly): Been working out 4 days a week. Can press 100 now.

Fancy Boots: My my my…So I bet you aren't sad to see the candy in the vending machines gone! I know how you love those Kitty Kat Crunchies…[*giggles*]

Bonaparte: Well, er [*indecipherable*]

Exasperation: Actually, Tracey, the revised vending-machine contents list is something of a problem for us.

Bonaparte: It is?

Exasperation: We are taking in approximately $100 less a month from that [*expletive deleted*] vending machine than we used to—$47 less on Kitty Kat Crunchies alone.

(throat clearing, coughing)

Fancy Boots: Well, I'm sure the revenues will pick up once people get used to the new offerings. The quinoa granola bars are really delicious!

Yeah, if you like dog biscuits

Exasperation: Well, if sales don't pick up fast, we won't have the funding for field-trip buses. Or to supply the punch and cookies like we always do for the grade 8 grad party.

Bonaparte: I'm sure we can find the money some-where. Can't we, Valerie?

Exasperation: We've already talked about this, Nat. Remember? We put the vending machines in the school in the first place because there was not enough money to fund our "desirables." And the funding from the board has gone down 12 percent since then.

Fancy Boots: We can't sacrifice the health of our children for a measly $100 a month, can we?

Exasperation: Fine. You tell the moms of those [expletive deleted] grade 8s that they won't be going to the [expletive deleted] annual end-of-year Major League Baseball game because there's no [expletive deleted] money for [expletive deleted] buses. And they should bring their own [expletive deleted] punch to the grade 8 dance while they're at it.

Fancy Boots: Tsk-tsk! Such negativity! Don't you know an optimistic attitude is half the battle? Parent Council can make up the shortfall. We'll just do another fundraiser!

Bonaparte: You mean another bake sale?

Fancy Boots: Why not? Who doesn't love a bake sale???

Travis gave me a knuckle-crunching fist bump. "I'll tell you who doesn't love another bake sale. Parents. You scored with this one, Darren. Big."

"You sure did," Lucinda said. It was lunchtime, and she was sitting as close to Travis as she could get without actually climbing into his lap. "My mother hates shelling out $10 for a cake it costs $1.99 to make. In actual fact, my mom hates all school fundraisers. The wrapping paper. The frozen cookie dough. The spring pansy sale. She says there's too much extra work involved. 'The G.D. second shift,' she calls it."

I threw my hands up in the air. "The paperwork alone!"

Lucinda giggled. "Exactly."

Travis edged away from Lucinda, but he was already halfway off the cafeteria bench. One more inch and he'd be on the floor. "So we've got our angle, then. Let parents know that if they don't put candy back in the vending machines, they'll be stuck doing more bake sales. And pansy sales. And…"

Lucinda bounced in her seat. "I can make a poster! For the meeting!" Her face got a goofy, glowing look. "If you want me to, Travis, that is."

Just a little creepy.

"Do you mind if I join you guys?" a silvery voice said in my ear.

It was Opal Vega. Only one of the prettiest girls at Preston Middle School. And co-founder of the Green Team, along with her twin sister, Amber.

Barf!

Evil baked goods

OPAL VEGA

Identifying Physical Features

- Porcelain skin
- Iridescent eyes
- Silvery voice

Known associates:
- ✿ Amber Vega – sister
- ✿ Outrage – mother

You gotta be kidding me!

Strengths: Devastating beauty. Gorgeous blue eyes, so gorgeous they can hypnotize you...

Weaknesses: None. She is pure perfection.

Interests: Environmental issues.

AMBER VEGA

Identifying Physical Features

- Eyes like yellow fire and a menacing glare

Towering height

Known associates:
- ✿ Opal Vega – sister
- ✿ Outrage – mother

AAAAAARGH!!!

Strengths: Xena-like strength. Hulk-like bad temper.

Weaknesses: Hulk-like bad temper.

Interests: Environmental issues.

The Loyal Opposition. So to speak.

"Er, sure," I croaked, sliding over to make room for her.

"I thought I heard you talking about Jason's candy initiative."

"Nooooo," Travis said. "We were talking about the *Band E* initiative. To get more kids taking up the electric tuba."

Opal gave Travis a cool smile. And an even cooler blue-eyed stare. "I was talking to Darren, Travis. Not you."

Travis's mouth opened and shut like a gasping fish. Lucinda bristled. I felt my ears go red.

"I know, I know. You all think I'm the enemy. The Green Team founder, right? Well, I've got news for you. The Green Team, especially some of the members by the name of Amber, can take their granola bars and stick 'em you know where."

"You fighting with your sister again?" Lucinda said.

"You really must be the smartest girl in grade 5," Opal said.

"Okay then," Lucinda said with a sniff.

"So I'm now on Team Waldo, as of this minute. If you'll have me, Darren."

I gulped and managed to squeak, "Sure."

Travis jumped to his feet. "First of all, there IS no Team Waldo. And second of all, no way! You can't let her in! It's like giving a saboteur the keys to the artillery magazine! She'll take whatever we say right back to the Green Team!"

"No I won't. I hate those double-crossing, backstabbing mean girls. I am finished with them. I mean it."

"So you say today. But tomorrow you'll all be, like, kissy-kissy and 'Omigod, luv your nail polish!' and 'BFFs 4ever!'" Travis said in his best girly-girl imitation.

Also a little creepy.

"You can't stay mad at Amber forever," Lucinda said. "You two live together. Not to mention the fact that your mother—who just happens to be the Parent Council V.P.—is 100 percent behind this no-candy thing."

"I'm moving in with my dad. I've had enough of both Amber and my mom."

"Really? You'd move out of your own house over this?" I said.

"Don't be an idiot, Darren. She's playing you!" Travis said.

"Well, not over this. But there's other...stuff," Opal said to me. Her beautiful opaline eyes began to shimmer.

Travis did a face palm. "Oh great. Now the crocodile tears. Fine. I'm out. Do what you want, Darren, but I am *finito*." And then he stalked off, muttering to himself.

"Wait, Travis!" Lucinda shouted, rising out of her seat.

"Let him go," I said.

Lucinda sighed heavily and sank back onto the bench.

"Don't feel bad, Lu," Opal said. "You don't need Travis's permission to make your cute little poster. I'll give you mine." Then she turned her big baby blues on me. "And while you're busy with that, Darren and I will make the flyers." Her delicate hand grazed my forearm. "You'll help me pass them out, too, won't you, D?"

ATTENTION, PRESTON PARENTS
Parent Council Wants Your $$$

Eliminating candy from the vending machines has resulted in a $1,200 shortfall in the Preston Middle School events budget. In order to make up the difference, Parent Council wants **YOU** to do:

MORE bake sales
MORE plant sales
MORE wrapping paper sales
MORE frozen cookie dough sales
MORE rummage sales

BUT there **IS** another solution. Vote **YES** at Tuesday evening's Parent Council meeting to the **Student Council's Vending Machine Initiative.** By restoring favorite treats to the vending machines, the shortfall can be eliminated with **no further fundraising on your part.**

⭐**WHEN:** This Tuesday, 7:30 PM
WHERE: Council Meeting Room, Second Floor,
South Wing, Preston Middle School

☑ Yes!

— *Free donuts and coffee!*

Messages   **T-Bone**

T, R u mad?

(......)

No.

Good. Can you come over?

y?

Strat and Tactics session.

I told u. I'm out.

Thought you weren't mad?

I'm not. But I don't trust Opal. She'll betray u, D.

Let me worry about O. I still need u 4 counterspy ops. Nothing to do with Green Team.

U mean Operation Blackmail Back?

Yes.

kk. B there in 5.

No—wait until dark.

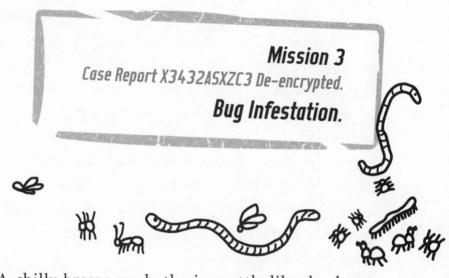

Mission 3
Case Report X3432ASXZC3 De-encrypted.
Bug Infestation.

A chilly breeze made the ivy rattle like dry bones. It whispered in my ear, "It's time."

My confederate was already in place. I could see his lanky form silhouetted in the upper-story window.

He flashed me three hand signals, confirming we had visual contact.

Three fingers, in the shape of a W. *Waldo.*

A slashing motion across his throat. *Mission abort.*

A circular motion by the side of his head.

Ha. Ha. Ha.

I, Dirk Daring, Secret Agent, am nothing if not efficient. I sent back a message using just *one* of my fingers.

As would be expected, I was expertly prepared for my night mission. Black pants, black shirt, black hat. I'd even smeared some black across my face.

I was as dark as the night around me, a racing cloud, a shadowed brow.

I was the Cat.

In my pockets—the tools of my trade. A coil of wire. Snippers. Lock picks. For not only was I Dirk Daring, Secret Agent, but I was also John "the Cat" Robie, the greatest cat burglar the world has ever known.

Why this double identity?

Because Dirk Daring, Secret Agent, knows that it takes a spy to catch a spy, but a thief to catch a thief.

And a Cat to catch a Rat.

The ivy whispered again. It was time.

I tested the tangled vines with my black-gloved hands. They were sturdy. Sturdy enough anyway.

I placed one black-shod foot carefully into the viny thicket. I put my full weight into it.

It held.

Step by step, inch by inch, I ascended the living ladder, as silent as the furtive feline who gave me his name.

Halfway there. Still no signal from my lookout. No one was approaching. Yet. But speed was of the essence. Speed and silence and cunning. Luckily, I, Dirk Daring, aka the Cat, had all those qualities. In spades.

I stretched upward, ever upward. Left foot, right foot. Left hand, right hand.

R-i-i-ippp!

The clump of vines I had seized tore away from the wall!

For one brief moment I dangled precariously in space. ~~My heart began to pou--~~ Yet my heart never altered its slow, steady rhythm. *Tha-dump. Tha-dump.* Dirk Daring, Secret Agent, did not fear heights. Nor did he fear spiders. Even when they crawled up his arm and into the collar of his shirt.

Ya right!

No, he did not.

Calmly, coolly, I plucked the errant arachnid from my neck and sent it spinning into the night. Calmly, coolly, I stretched my supple fingers toward another clump of ivy. When they made purchase, I tugged with all my considerable might. Yes—this clump would hold.

I resumed my steady climb.

Left foot, right foot. Left hand, right hand.

Five feet. Eight feet. Almost there.

Just one more catlike creep, and my fingers caressed the windowsill. Another quick-footed half step, and my nose felt the kiss of smooth, dark glass.

I had arrived at my destination.

Now, to slip inside.

The Cat needs no glass cutter, no hammer, to effect entry. For the Cat has cleverness. The cat has craftiness. And the Cat has modern technology.

I ♥ Wi-Fi

I carefully drew the wireless microphone from my pocket. Kissed it. Because a better, more furtive surveillance device there could not be. I had tested and retested it for range and effectiveness through glass. Naturally, it had met every hurdle with (Wi)Fi-ing colors. It would pick up a flea's fart through 6 inches of solid steel if my mission required it. Luckily, it did not.

I switched the mic on. The LED on its side flashed red.

I whispered into it, "The Cat is on the Rat."

The light in my bedroom window flicked on and off.

T-Bone had heard my message. *All systems go.*

Now all I had to do was stick the mic onto Waldo's window, and I'd be privy to his every conversation, his deepest, darkest secrets. Ugh.

I peered through the glass. There it was—Waldo's T-ball trophy collection. Nestled up against the window, lower left-hand corner. Festooned with a crown of dust even thicker than his head.

I lined up the spongy, double-sided tape on the back of the mic with the left edge of the window frame, right behind the Most Improved Player trophy. There the mic would be undetectable. Just like me, Dirk Daring, Secret Agent. Hiding in plain sight.

I peeled off the tape's paper strip. I squished the mic to the window. It stuck.

"The Cat is in the Hat," I whispered into the mic. The lights in the window of my room flicked off and on.

Message received.

The lights flicked off again. Then on. Then off.

Approaching enemy!

My Cat senses sprang into high alert.

There was no time to lose.

Before I could leap into action, even more lights flicked on. This time, the lights in Waldo's room!

I froze, my face still pressed to the cold glass.

But the Cat does not panic. The Cat waits patiently for the Rat to enter his trap.

I ducked my head so only my eyes showed over the windowsill. With bated breath, I observed my target.

Through the glass, I saw Waldo toss his backpack onto his bed. Then he sprawled out next to it on his back, like a dying lobster.

He yawned.

A tonsil-exposing yawn.

He scratched his head.

An armpit-exposing scratch.

And he burped.

A rich, fruity burp.

Such was my adversary. A pathetically base creature, completely lacking the refinement of the Cat.

Just as the Rat began picking his nose, I slid down the ivy and melted into the night.

Travis was wandering around my bedroom, picking up and putting down all my stuff. Noises from Waldo's room came through my computer's speakers at steady but infrequent intervals.

"All he ever does is burp and fart, man! So boring. *And* gross."

"Welcome to my world. He sometimes does take a break though. To torture small animals."

Travis snickered. "So you're calling yourself a small animal now? Oh, right—you're 'the Cat.' Forgive me." He snickered again.

"Go ahead. Laugh if you want. The Cat has patience enough for your jibes. *And* for Waldo to do something interesting."

"Better you than me."

Another juicy belch blared from my computer's speakers.

"Ugh, that one was disgusting! That's it! I'm outta here."

"Wait! Catch."

Travis bobbled the binder I tossed to him. Then, when he had it firmly in hand, he held it at arm's length. Studying it. His eyes were jumbo olives.

"What the—! You're giving me your precious spy journal?"

"Simple safety precaution. If the book is at your house, Waldo can't get his clutches on it again."

"B-but Darren! What will you do without it? Isn't it, like, your favorite teddy bear and favorite rubber ducky all wrapped up in leatherette?"

"Ha. And ha. It's just a binder, Travis."

"As if. But how will you manage without your daily dose of Dear Diary? Will you start twitching or something? I don't want to have to perform CPR on you if you seize."

I practiced the Zen of Espionage: Slow, even breathing.

In.

Out.

In.

Out.

"Your concern is touching," I finally replied. "But misplaced. I still have this"—I held up a pen—"and this"—I held up a package of loose-leaf paper. "I can write up my mission notes wherever I want. I'll deliver them to you to add to the permanent file when needed. So trust me, I'll survive just fine."

Travis shook his head slowly. "You got everything all worked out, don't you?"

"Take care of the binder, okay? I'm trusting you with my life, Travis. You know that, don't you?"

Another burp rolled from the computer's speakers.

"Yeah yeah yeah. I've got your back." He chuckled again. "Have fun with the Burperator. Can't wait to read your mission notes about this 'episode.' Sure they'll be 'a gas.'"

He paused on his way out the door and gave me a crooked grin.

"And by the way, Dirk, next time, for your face, you might want to use something less…long-lasting…than a Sharpie."

Transcript of phone message left by Mrs. Helen Troy on Preston Middle School's voice mail. 11/09 08:31:16.

Hi. This is Helen Troy calling. Darren Dirkowitz's mom. He's in Miss Templeton's class, Room—what's your room number again, Darren?—Room 5. He won't be in to school today. He has a painful rash on his face. It's pretty bad, red and raw, like he scrubbed half his skin away! No other symptoms—hope it's not contagious! Will keep you posted. Thanks.

There is no mission too challenging for Dirk Daring, Secret Agent. But some are more delicate than others.

Some require split-second timing.

Some require the reflexes of a cat, or the unflappability of a hawk.

And some require winning the trust of others.

And then betraying that trust.

For there are times, in the shadow world, when betrayal is loyalty. And places, in the shadow world, where evil is goodness.

Dusk was falling. The footpaths were emptying of civilians. I, Dirk Daring, checked my surroundings.

Left, right. Left, right. No one was watching. I unlocked my conveniently located but secure hidey-hole and removed my mission gear from within. Then, nonchalantly, I sauntered toward my designated mission coordinates.

Unobserved, I slipped inside.

The room in which I found myself was dark. Empty. Silent as the grave, except for the *drip drip drip* of a persistent leak.

I carefully removed my weapon from my backpack. Prepared it to fire.

Unexpectedly, it made a peculiar rattle. The knocking together of old bones. I quickly stilled my weapon to silence it. Luckily, no one else had heard. For Dirk Daring, Secret Agent, would allow no witnesses to his dark doings. None to hear, none to see, none to live.

It was time—now or never. I aimed my weapon at my target, lining it up with incredible precision. And I struck.

Shzzzt! Shzzzt shzzzt shtzzzt! Shzzt! Shzzzt shzzzt! Seven quick, perfect shots.

Each left a distinctive mark. Together, they created a very specific pattern. It was one I had practiced, over and over, till I could reproduce it with exactitude.

Every time.

In any place.

No matter what.

What was this mysterious pattern? I can only reveal that it contained a message. A clearer-than-clear message.

One I knew my intended recipient would receive.

I knew, too, that my message would garner a swift and immediate response.

Strike = Counterstrike.

Action = Reaction.

Tit = Tat.

I paused for a moment to admire my handiwork. It was sheer brilliance. Then I stowed my weapon and moved on.

Opal met me at my locker.

"I'm SOOO glad you didn't miss school today. Travis said you had some icky rash that turned your face all oozy red and purple yesterday."

I felt my face turn redder than ever. "It wasn't that bad."

Ooooh ~~~ Darren loves Opal! ♡

"Good. And you look almost normal now. Except that you're blushing. Gee, you look cute when you blush, Darren!"

I thought I might just melt into a puddle of red-and-purple shame, right there and then. But I couldn't escape, not via liquid runoff shame melt or any other method. Opal was still talking. And when Opal talked, you listened.

"What do you think of the flyers? I finished them last night. Used up all the printer ink. So?"

She stuck the stack of flyers under my nose.

They were excellent.

"Aw, Darren, so sweet of you to say so! But now it's time to get to work. We have to hand out all of these sheets—every single one of them—to every kid we can before the buses leave. I'm counting on you to hit everybody I miss." She put her hand on my sleeve. "You ready?"

"Ready!" I hiccupped.

I followed Opal to the front doors, where the buses were already pulling up. Kids were milling about and goofing around. Some had already started getting on the buses.

"Quick! You start there!" She shoved a handful of flyers at me and pushed me toward the first school bus. "I'll take the next one!"

I climbed the bus stairs.

"Step right up! Take a flyer and get candy back in school! Give these little babies to your parents!

Don't forget! Bring your folks to Parent Council night if you want candy back in the vending machines! Come and lend your support!"

I was having so much fun, I almost forgot I was doing this candy thing for Waldo. Because, of course, I was now doing it for Opal too. And Opal smelled a heck of a lot better than Waldo. I'd never seen Opal picking her nose either.

As I made my way through the bus, kids grabbed for the flyers. There was a lot of excited jabbering.

"Awesome! You mean we can get candy back again?"

"All right! Whose idea was this anyway? Jason's? Wow!"

"Nice work, D!"

I was feeling pretty ace until a foot jutted out across the aisle and blocked my way. A very big foot. In a very fancy running shoe. With pink glitter on it.

Amber Vega. Opal's sister. Green Team co-founder. Archenemy of candy.

"What exactly is this?" She grabbed one of the flyers and scanned it rapidly. Her eyes narrowed. Her mouth dropped open as she read the last line. "This is Opal's handwriting!!! That little scheming, two-timing backstabber!"

Amber got to her feet, and when she did, she towered over me. Even though Amber and Opal are twins, they aren't identical. In fact, they are almost exact opposites. Where Opal is small and delicate, Amber is a wildebeest: fierce, athletic and tough as nails. Where Opal's eyes are palest Wedgewood blue, Amber's glow like yellow fire.

It was rumored that Amber also possessed the most powerful left uppercut of anyone in grade 5.

I didn't know what to say or do, so I stalled.

Can you say DEATH WISH???

"Excuse me? Are you talking about yourself again? That's not very polite."

Amber ignored me. With great ceremony, she ripped the flyer into little bitty bits. Then she stared down the rest of the kids on the bus. "The meeting tonight is canceled. Do you hear me? Any of your parents who go will be wasting their time. And I'll be there, at the door, to advise them of that fact. And to see who exactly shows up." She cracked her knuckles. Slowly.

"Hey! That's voter intimidation!" I said. "Cut that out!"

She put her nose to mine. "Get off this bus, Darren. Now."

I put my hands up. "Whoa, I'm just doing a little service for our school prez."

She gritted her teeth. "Get off the bus, Darren. And when you see my so-called sister, tell her I'll be waiting for her. Tonight. To have a little sisterly 'chat.' Got it?"

"Yeah yeah yeah. Remember, folks! Parent Council meeting tonight! Come one, come all! It's going to be quite the showdown! Candy versus granola! Amber versus Opal! Don't miss it!"

I had a big grin on my face as I swung down the bus steps.

This couldn't be any better. As soon as word got out that there could be a big ugly fight between Opal and Amber at the meeting, I knew interest would shoot up. We'd make our goal, easily-peasily. Unless something unexpected happened, that is.

The Parent Council meeting room was packed. Jammed to the gills. People were standing in the hallway, unable to get through the doors.

"Wow!" Lucinda said. "All these people came out to vote for candy?"

"Don't be such a dweeb," Amber said. "Most of them came to support *us*. Because intelligent people know health and physical fitness matter."

"Oh, stuff it. You don't care about health. You just like bossing people around."

Waldo got between them. "Ladies! Ladies!" He wore a big fat cheese-eating grin on his ugly mug, making it even uglier. "We can agree to disagree and still behave civilly. Can't we?"

"Mind your own beeswax, Jason," Amber said.

"Certainly. *After* we get candy reinstated. Shall we?" He extended his arm, ushering the two girls into the meeting room.

Opal was suddenly at my side. "Oooh—she's one pissed Vega."

"Well, she should be—we're gonna win. Thanks to your flyers."

She beamed up at me. I felt a thousand feet tall.

Travis came around the corner with his mom. He'd told me earlier that his mom didn't give two hoots about candy, but she sure wanted to see Fancy Boots get a drubbing. Apparently a lot of the other moms felt the same way—there was a giddy, gossipy buzz in the room, and it was getting shriller and shriller.

If I'd been smart, I'd have set odds and taken bets on the outcome.

Fancy Boots banged a gavel on the lectern. "This meeting is now called to order. It's so amazing to see such a big turnout tonight. I understand many of you have taken a special interest in our final item on the agenda: the motion to reinstate candy in the vending ma—"

Her words were cut off by loud cheers and boos. Not all of them coming from us kids.

"Order! Order! So let's get through the rest of the items on our agenda as quickly as possible."

Fancy Boots smiled brightly, but her forehead bore a deep double crease down the middle. She cleared her throat about 12 times, and finally the crowd began to settle. She began rattling off some information about new staffing models for the library.

I stopped listening about half a word in—instead, I had my eye on Amber. She was glaring at Opal with a hard, hot stare I knew could only mean trouble. Every fiber of my being went into high alert. My instincts, honed by my secret identity as Dirk Daring, Secret Agent, told me to stand guard. To keep Opal safe.

While I was considering which was the better option—throwing myself like a human shield over Opal or taking out Amber with my karate chop's incredible speed and pinpoint accuracy—I felt a hand grip my neck from behind.

Waldo.

I tried to wrench myself free, but I couldn't. His grasp was as strong as his body odor, and just as objectionable.

"Lemme go!" I hissed.

"Sure, little bro." He released me with a simultaneous shove that almost knocked me to my knees. "Sorry. Don't always know my own strength. I just wanted to find out the status of that other matter. The one we discussed."

"It's done. Now leave me alone."

"No can do, Dirk." He laughed an evil laugh. "You see, I need you. Just as much as you need me."

And then he was gone, leaving me to ponder the meaning of his words. Because as far as I was concerned, I needed Waldo about as much as I needed a crevice in the cranium. Less, actually.

PRESTON PRESTIGE

RE-TREAT!!!

The People Have Spoken and Said, "Give Us Our Candy!"

BY OPAL VEGA, STAFF REPORTER

Student Body President Jason Arsenico pleased with his victory.

In a stunning reversal of existing school policy, the motion to reinstate candy in Preston Middle School's vending machines was passed by a vote of 27-21 at last night's Parent Council meeting.

Student Body President Jason Arsenico, who co-authored the motion, said, "We're thrilled by the results. Our action wasn't really about candy though. It was about freedom of personal choice. Do we want to live in a society where a select group of people, with their own narrow agenda, can determine for all of us what we do, think or eat?"

The "select group" Mr. Arsenico referred to is the Green Team, the student group that initiated the original motion to ban candy from the machines. Their mission: to instill healthier eating habits in the Preston student body, whether they like it or not. Amber Vega, one of the co-founders of the Green Team, could not be reached for comment.

In general, the student body seems delighted that favorite treats like Nanaimo Bites and Kitty Kat Crunchies will be back on the menu. Chants of "Candy rocks" and "Down with quinoa" reverberated through the town streets when the meeting broke up.

The popular treats should be back in the machines by the start of Winter Term, and will sell for a very reasonable $1 each. Sales from the vending machines will go toward the grade 8 class trip and graduation fund.

Amber Vega, co-founder of the Green Team, disapproved of the voting results.

We'd just finished singing the national anthem when the intercom buzzed like a sick fly. A moment later, Ms. Wycoff's delightful nasal tones reverberated through the loudspeaker. "Miss Templeton, send Travis Sendak down to the principal's office. Please."

Travis pointed to himself with a "Who, me?" look on his face.

A whisper ran through the class like a bad oyster.

What had Travis done to get "The Call"?

As he passed by my desk on his death march, I nodded to him in a silent show of support. He gave me a "thanks, dude" wink and was gone.

The clock ticked.

Tick. Tick. Tick.

No Trav.

Tick. Tick. Tick.

Gone waaaay too long.

A lump of fear congealed in my gut. *Maybe something really bad had happened, like to his parents. Maybe—*

Travis would be fine. He was *always* fine.

Tick. Tick. Tick.

Only 3 more ticks until the bell would ring for lunch.

Tick. Tick.

The classroom door swung open and banged against the wall.

Travis stood in the open doorway. His face and eyes were red, and his lips were bone white.

The whole class gasped as one just as the lunch bell rang. Travis spun on his heel and was gone.

I ran like mad after him, but I was already too late.

I finally found him in north bathroom 4B. He was sitting in one of the stalls, his elbows on his knees, head in his hands. I gaped at him. Was he producing a confidential, ahem, memo?

No. Impossible.

So what was he doing, sitting on the can? At school?

I tried to make light of the situation. "Dude, you're supposed to pull your pants down before using the throne," I said.

Travis gave me a withering look, then returned his head to his hands.

"What happened?" No reply. "Come on, it can't be that bad…"

"Oh yeah? Detention. FOR A WHOLE MONTH. For something I DIDN'T do!"

I put my hand on his shoulder. "Spill it. Before it eats your guts from the inside out."

His eyes flicked to mine and he nodded. In a somber tone, he described how Principal Bonaparte had sat him down in the execution chair and fixed his beady seagull eyes on him.

HISSSSSSSS

Travis gave me his best, syrupy impression of Big B. *"Why don't you tell me about it, son?* I had no clue what he was talking about. So he gets all pissy. *I've had just about enough of your bad attitude, Mr. Sendak.* He marched me down the hall to the south bathroom. Pushed me into a stall. Practically shoved my face into it."

"What? A toilet?"

"Don't be a dweeb. The *door*. There was a tag there. *My* Surfer Dude guy!"

I swallowed hard. "You drew Surfer Dude on the bathroom stall? What were you thinking, Travis? Dumb dumb dumb…" I shook my head.

He gave me a deadeye. And a severely curled lip.

I swear! "'Course I didn't do it. I got framed, man! And now I've got to write a stupid apology to the stupid school janitor and serve one whole stupid month in the can."

I mumbled something sympathetic, but Travis was beyond hearing.

"Who'd do that? Who'd want to screw me over like that?"

I raised my eyebrows. "No one. Not that I can think of. Er…other than Waldo, that is."

Travis gave me a sharp look. "Waiiiitttt…do you think it was Waldo?"

I lifted my hands in helplessness. "How should I know?"

"Because you live with the psycho? And you've bugged his room?"

"Can't help you there. He hasn't copped to art forgery. Not out loud anyway. Of course, that doesn't mean he didn't do it. I wouldn't put anything past him."

Travis drummed his fingers on his knees. He shrugged one shoulder, then the other, like he was shaking off especially persistent flies. Then he gave me such a desperate, pleading look, it pierced me to the core. "Will you find out for me, Darren? I mean, can you spy on him for me while you're spying for you?"

"Sure. Hey—that's what friends are for. Now can we please get out of this stall before I get the urge to draw a pair of spy eyes on the door?"

He smiled at the thought. "That's funny. I could use that idea in my next installment of *Surfer Dude*."

I waved my arm and bowed. Sort of—it's pretty hard to wave and bow in a toilet stall. There was a near-clunking of heads.

"Feel free. I share with you the fruits of my brilliant imagination. Free of charge."

I waited for Travis, kicking at dried-out clumps of crab-grass in front of the school, for a whole hour. Because hey, that's what friends are for too.

Finally, he emerged through the double doors. Head down, hands heavy, skate shoes dragging along the pavement with an audible *shlump shlump shlump*.

"So. How'd day one of detention go?"

He just gave me a look.

"Come on, it couldn't have been *that* bad," I said, trotting beside him.

I got another look. One even colder, if possible.

"Whoa—they must have done a number on you in there. Did they bamboo-shoot you? Travis! Talk to me! What's my name? What's my name?"

Travis shrugged my hand off his wrist, but a ghost of a smile crossed his lips.

"Dirk the Dork. Now leave me alone."

"Come on. Tell me what happened."

"Nothing. They just made me write *I will not deface school property* 100 times." He held up his left hand. Clawed. "I'll never play piano now, never again."

"Since when do you play piano?"

I got a look that could freeze gonads.

"So that's it? Nobody sawed off your leg? Or threatened your mother?"

Travis shook his head. "That new grade 8 teacher, Miss Robinette, is in charge of detention these days. Apparently she's really mean, and no one wants to mess with her—not even the Detention Gang."

He trudged along beside me. "I still can't believe anyone would frame me like this. Like, what did I ever do to anybody?"

We heard a loud snort. Very close by. Both of us practically jumped out of our epidermi.

It was Opal. She was suddenly *there*. At Travis's elbow.

"Jeez Louise, where the heck did you come from?" Travis squeaked.

Opal shrugged. "Who, me? Nowhere. I was just hanging here, minding my own business, and you two practically ran me over. You should watch where you're going."

She fell in step alongside us. "I couldn't help but overhear you guys. Talking about who might have it in for you, Travesty—I mean Travis." She gave him a sideways glance. "How about, like, everyone?"

Travis didn't answer her.

"What are you talking about?" I said.

"Not this again!" Travis clutched both sides of his head. "Don't pay any attention to her, Darren! I told you, she's a saboteur. Out to get us. Playing both sides of the fence."

Opal smiled even more broadly. I saw the tip of one of her pearly white canines flash brightly in the sun. "Of course that's what you'd say, Travis. After all, who'd know more about double-dealing than you?" She turned to me. "You know you shouldn't trust this guy, right? I mean, I know you two have been friends for, like, forever, but he's not exactly straight up with you. Is he?" Her eyes swung back to Travis. "He's made a lot of enemies around these parts."

"Oh yeah? Like who?" I said.

"*Adios*, Opal," Travis said, stepping up his pace.

Opal laughed. "Go ahead. Let your *good pal* Darren fight your battles for you while you run away. You won't be able to hide. Especially up there in detention..."

She laughed again, right in his face.

I could see Travis's cheeks getting redder by the second. If Opal had been a guy, he would have popped her one already.

Opal flipped a waterfall of blond hair over her shoulder. She gave him one more smug smile. A cat licking cream. Then she looked at me. "You know I'm not a gossip girl, no matter what *he* says. So I'll let Travis be the one to tell you all about it. Right, Travis?"

That smirk again.

She gave me a little fingertippy wave over her shoulder. "See you tomorrow, Darren."

And she blew me a kiss. ——→ Get a grip!

My jaw dropped open like it had a fish hook in it and the line had snapped tight.

Flappety flap flap. Just like that, I felt myself being reeled into the kill bucket.

Strangely, it didn't seem bad at all, not with Opal holding the fishing rod…

Travis tugged my sleeve, yanking me out of my trance. "Don't fall for her crap. I already told you, she's a liar and a schemer. You shouldn't believe a word she says."

"Yeah yeah yeah." I was walking like a man in a dream. My head in the ozone, my feet…somewhere else.

We walked along in silence then. Travis was fuming inwardly—smoke didn't need to pour from his ears to make that clear.

Meanwhile, my own brain attempted to reboot itself.

Eventually, it came up with a red-alert warning. Flagging one unexplainable oddity.

Opal *hated* Travis.

Like I care! But *why?*

Suddenly, I was back. Brain online. In control. Inquiring.

"Trav? What are you not telling me? There is something, isn't there?"

He rounded on me. "Oh great. She's blowing steam up your butt, but you're still going to believe her over me? Your best friend? Nice, Darren. Nice."

"No—I don't!" I said, letting my hands dangle at my sides. "I'm just...just...confused. That's all."

"What's there to be confused about? You trust me or you don't. You believe her lies. Or you don't."

I didn't say anything. I just stood there like a fire hydrant waiting for the dog.

"Fine. Go ahead. Be 'confused.' But don't forget, I'm confused too—like about who exactly set me up for detention. And now I'm thinking maybe it was you. You and Opal."

"What? That's nuts!"

Travis's whole body stiffened.

"Darren. Look at me. Come on. Right in the eye. Look me right in the eye and tell me you and Opal had nothing to do with getting me detention."

I looked him straight in the eye. "Opal and I didn't get you detention. Okay? Jeez, I can't believe you would even think that."

Travis still had his eyes on me. It was unbearable, the mistrust I saw there.

Truly unbearable.

I stuffed my hands in my pockets and started walking away.

"Okay. OKAY! Forget it! Look, I'm just tired. And mad. And frustrated. And that...that...Opal is getting under my skin. I can't believe you want anything to do with her."

I stopped walking. Gave him a big fat grin.

"In case you haven't noticed, dude, Opal's really pretty. Okay?"

Travis's shoulders relaxed. He smiled too, a crooked, apologetic smile.

"Pretty shmitty. You're forgetting she's the enemy, Dirk. Sent to niggle out your secrets. Prey on your weaknesses. And turn you into cow patty."

"That's a pile of crap and you know it," I said, making us both laugh out loud.

Shhh—someone is listening.

Watch yourself—someone is spying.

Always, always, there is the narrowed eye. The quivering ear. For your adversary is taking note of all you do. Watching for that one word slip, listening for that one careless whoopsy, that gives you away. Watching, and waiting...

But alas, discovery equals death in the shadow world. There is no respawn. Just you, your failure and the endless sleep.

Fear not. You will not be discovered. Not, that is, if you are Dirk Daring, Secret Agent.

For Dirk Daring has thoroughly mastered the arts of subterfuge and secrecy.

His model? The purloined letter, hidden in plain sight.

His muse? The incredible art forger Han van Meegeren.

Carefully, I collect the precious chemical compound that I will use for my "ink." It is not easy to gather, not without attracting attention. Nor is it pleasant. Nevertheless, I proceed. For nothing stands in the way of Dirk Daring, Secret Agent, when he has struck a plan, and the plan is sound.

The ink is a pale fluid that will disappear once it dries. In its place will be an invisible text—one that requires arcane knowledge to bring it back to readability. A knowledge only known to Dirk Daring and the one to whom he confides the secret.

No one must know of my covert actions. Therefore, I use ultimate discretion and a steady hand to obtain my ink. And carefully, carefully, I transport it to my bolt-hole—a secret, forbidden location. There, I have hidden my specially prepared writing implements, crafted from a seagull feather; they are taped to the underside of the sofa. None but the cat will espy them. None but the Cat would suspect...

I look left, then right. Left, right. No one is watching. No one is listening.

I store the ink in the ancient desk's drawer and wait until the bowels of the night. Then, and only then, when no one stirs, not even a Waldo, I creep from my bed. Creep to my bolt-hole. Retrieve my pen.

I use my cell phone as a flashlight. At first, its small, bright screen blinds me, but I let my eyes adjust to its glow. There's just enough luminosity to allow me to see what I am doing. But not enough to alert unwelcome noseypants of my presence. Good to go.

I slide a bare sheet of paper from the desk. I withdraw the cup of pale ink from the drawer and place it carefully, carefully, on the desk. It would not do to spill even one drop of the precious elixir.

I dip the pen. I write, and dip, and write. As quickly as I can, I jot down my confidential report. Dip again.

It is slow, laborious work. The nearly colorless fluid dries and fades even as I write, leaving nothing but a ghostly trail on the paper. I cannot check my work, so every letter must be perfect from the get-go. Naturally, Dirk Daring, Secret Agent, does not err—I have precluded the possibility by memorizing my memorandum, word for word, beforehand. It will be accurate. To the point. A model of efficient covert communication. A masterpiece of missioncraft.

At last. It is done. The message written. The ink, a memory trace.

But still my mission is not complete. Now I must disguise my sheet of paper so it does not look like what it is: a blank sheet of paper. Deception within deception—the hallmark of my genius.

But how will I transform the sheet of blank paper into something "other"? Will I write upon it in "regular" ink, deceiving casual observers with an alternate, innocuous message—"milk, potatoes, toilet paper?" No—because that is too obvious a move for Dirk Daring. Better to make my piece of paper not look like a piece of paper at all.

I will make it a sculpture. A toy. A delicate artwork for the delight and amusement of small, easily amused children. No one will suspect such an innocent plaything will contain a secret message of the highest import.

I fold the paper in half, then in half again. Squash to make a square. Turn and squash again. Fold it twice, then swivel and flatten to make a kite shape. Repeat on the other side. Bend up one "leg." Bend up the other "leg." Crimp the end of one "leg." Now it is a beak, not a leg.

Voilà. My masterpiece is complete—an origami bird. That flaps its wings when you pull its tail.

It is this subtle subterfuge I will bring with me to the designated meet. There I will pass my message on to a confederate—an agent called T-Bone. T-Bone will then magic the message away to his own bolt-hole. Then, and only then, will he perform the arcane procedure that is necessary to reveal the message so he can enter its information into his massive secret database.

It is imperative that none but T-Bone come into possession of this priceless resource. So fly away, little bird! For on your wings you carry all the hope of a better world.

Pee-ewww!

"Oh, that birdie is so cute! I looooove origami!" Lucinda cooed. "Can I try flapping it?"

"No!" My voice came out excessively harsh. "Er, it's delicate, that's all. I made it for Travis."

"Aw, isn't that special," Amber said.

"It's not like that," I said, scrambling. "You see, Travis is making this thousand-crane thing. For his cousin. She's in the hospital. With, um, Dalmation Pekinisia! A terrible disease. The cranes are for good luck. And healing."

Lucinda turned her face to Travis. "That's so…sad!"

"Doggone sad." Amber tossed her head and laughed—a vulgar bark of a laugh.

"And sooo sweet of you too, Travis!" Lucinda's big cow eyes started to swim. She clasped her hands together; I fully expected her to moo any second. GROSS!

"Riiiight." Travis yanked at his collar like it was too tight. "Fine." He waggled his fingers at me. "Give it, then."

I gently flipped him the bird. Travis bobbled it in his right hand for a second. Then it came to rest in his palm. He peered at it closely. His nose crinkled.

"What did you make this with, dude? Toilet paper? 'Cause it reeks like the boys' peebox." He waved his left hand in front of his nose. "Stinkybird."

I felt the tips of my ears redden.

"If it has a slight gamey fragrance, it's because I used A1-quality origami paper. It's 100 percent organic and all natural." I tried to send him a discreet but clear 'shut up' signal by waggling my left eyebrow, but Travis ignored it. His lip twitched.

"Right again. You can tell me all about its organic *pee*-urfume over lunch. I have a *pee*-strami sandwich. What did you bring? *Pee*-nut butter?" He laughed at his own bad jokes, then shoved the bird into the dark maw of his desk, pushing it as far as it could go with the eraser end of his pencil. "I think I'll handle it as little as possible, in any case. Since it's so 'delicate.'"

"Can you make a birdie for me, Darren? Please?" Lucinda said.

"And me?" Amber batted her eyes. "I'm sure you have another *pee*ce of paper somewhere, Darren." Then she guffawed, a giant Amber guffaw.

"How about I make you a muzzle?"

She was just forming her fingers into a fist when Miss Templeton called the class to order.

New Message

Send   Sent 11/16 06:31:12

To: Tsendak@goggle.com

Subject: Top secret/ultra-classified/delete after reading

Instructions for Revealing Invisible Ink

1. Unfold.

2. Hold paper over heat source.

3. Message will be revealed.

4. Caution! Do not hold message too close to heat source!

Re: Document Transfer 3242hut.
Transcript of De-encrypted Message
Code Name Birdy Birdy.

Transcript of surveillance mission—Operation Listen-in. 20:32.
Audio recording via listening device #1.000000
Location: Window mount/Waldo's bedroom
20:32:00›› 20:32:58

Hisssssssssssssssssssssssssssssssssssscracklehisssssssssss
ssssss ssssssssssssssssssssssssscracklecrackle hiss
sssssssssssssssssssssssssssssssssssssssssssssburppppphis
sssburpetyburphissssssssssssss
20:33:00›› 20:33:42
(cell phone ring tone: Birdy Birdy Song.)
Rustlerustlerustle

Waldo: You again...What now?...Look—I already did what you
asked...Fine. But this is the last time. I mean it.
Rustle rustle rustle
‹faint sound of laughter.›
 20:34:00›› 21:30:00
Hisssssssssssssssssssssssssssssssssssscracklehisssssssssss
ssssssssssssssssssssssssssssssssscracklecrackle hisssssss
ssssssssssssssssssssssssssssssssssssssssburpppppphisssshiss
ssssssssssssssssssssssssssssssssssssssssssssssssssssssss
ssssssssssssssssssssssssssssssssssssssssssssssssssssss
sssssssssssssssssssssssssssssssssssssssssssssssssssss
sssssssssssssssssss

We met to discuss the matter in hand after school. After T was out of detention.

Location: My room.

"Any idea who he was talking to?" Travis asked me, still shrugging off his coat.

"Oh, I have an idea. Or two. I'm sure I recognized that laugh."

Travis's neck stiffened. "What are you saying, Darren?"

"Chill, dude. I didn't mean you."

"Oh. Sorry. For a second I thought...So who *do* you think it was?" He kicked back on my bed and cracked his knuckles one at a time. *Pop pop pop. Pop pop pop. Poppety pop pop.* I did my best to ignore it, but it wasn't easy. *Pop pop.* He had more knuckles, it seemed, than freckles.

"Who do you know that has a laugh you can hear clear through a cell phone?"

He cracked a grin. But then his brows collapsed into each other, forming a fuzzy pair of vulture's wings over his dark eyes. "But wait—what the heck would she be calling Waldo for?"

"Well said, Monsieur Le T-Bone. What exactly, indeed!" I held up one finger and rocked forward in my chair until I was practically nose to nose with Travis. "And even more important, what could she be holding over our own dear archenemy step-psychopath?"

Travis's smile grew even broader. "Blackmail. Extortion. Not what I would have imagined as her style. I'm suddenly liking her a lot better!"

"You are so twisted."

"Thank you." Travis dipped his head. "But really— this is some choice data, Darren. Nice work. I hereby promote you to chief espionage officer. In training."

When the ensuing wrestle-mania session ended, we still had a problem at hand.

"Fact," I said. "Waldo has a secret.

"Fact: His secret is known to another and is being used for extortion and blackmail.

"Fact: We do not know what said secret is, and if we did, we could have even more valuable information at our disposal. We might even be able to shut the Waldo Wagon down for good."

"Sounds like a mission statement to me, bro," Travis said, giving me one last noogie.

My mother was calling—no, not calling—screaming my name. "Get right down here. This INSTANT!"

I scrambled, trying to assemble my very best innocent youngster face. I wondered what the heck I was going to have to talk myself out of this time.

I didn't have to wait long to find out. When I skidded into my mom's office, she was leaning against her old desk, one arm across her body, the other holding my precious ink. Which I, apparently, had neglected to spirit out of my bolt-hole when I'd finished my business with it.

Oopsy.

"What is *this* doing in my drawer?" Her eyes would have shot lightning bolts if she'd been plugged in properly, but my mom was too mad to read her own operating manual. Lucky me.

"Sorry, lemme take that from you. I can explain." I reached for the jar.

"You'd better, and fast, tell me how a container of urine wound up in a room to which you are expressly forbidden admission."

"Mom, it's really very simple—here, come on. Give it to me."

"Talk. Now." She raised the jar up in the air, away from my grasping hands.

"Come on, Mom. Be careful with that! It's not what you think!"

"Oh, so it's not pee, then?"

"Well, er, no, I mean, yes, but…"

I grabbed again for the jar.

Our hands collided.

Catastro-pee!!!

Transcript of phone message left by Mrs. Helen Troy on Preston Middle School's voice mail. UB4OU2 De-encrypted. 11/18 08:32:25.

Hi. This is Helen Troy calling. Darren Dirkowitz's mom. He's in Miss Templeton's class, Room 5. He won't be coming in to school today. He got something in his eye last night and today he has pinkeye, so I'm going to keep him home until it's cleared up.
Thanks.

Hahaha peeenk eye!!

Travis could not stop laughing.

"Are you done yet?" I said, squeezing my pillow into a small, compact knot. Squeeze, release. Squeeze, release.

"Don't think so." His eyes streamed, and he clutched at his belly and rocked back and forth. "I think I just might *pee* myself!"

"Get the heck off my bed first, then." I shoved him off, hard, with my foot. He fell to the floor, still laughing, still clutching his sides.

"And now you have *pee*nk eye!!!" he howled, rolling around like a pea in a salad spinner.

"Call me when you are done being a cretin." The sound of the door slamming behind me made the walls shake.

I took a long, slow walk around the block. I needed it, to let my anger dissipate. Okay, so it *was* pretty stupid, I admit it, to get pee in your own eye. Day-old pee, no less. But Travis didn't have to be so *schmucky* about it, did he? A little ribbing, sure—I could take that. But being laughed at was not exactly my idea of a fun way to spend an afternoon. Besides, my eye hurt like a bugger. I wanted a little sympathy, not humiliation.

The walk helped though—I could feel my heart rate gradually slow and my rage fade. This was Travis we were talking about, after all. My best buddy. It wasn't the first time he'd pushed my buttons. But we always worked it out.

He'd realize he'd gone too far this time. He'd let it drop and pretend like it never happened.

I could be cool with that. We'd go on like before. Friends again. The whole pee thing just so much— ha-ha—water under the bridge.

When I got back home, Travis was sitting just where I'd left him, on the floor.

I plunked myself down across from him. "You finished your laugh fest yet?"

Travis didn't look at me. He just sat there, staring at his feet, like a big lump. Regret was written all over him.

I breathed a sigh of relief. Knowing he felt bad made it easier for me to forgive and forget. I could be gracious and move on.

"I'll take that as an apology," I said.

"I think it's *you* who owes me the apology, dude."

What????

Anger bloomed in me all over again. I felt my fists tighten into hard knots.

"For what? For making you laugh so hard you got a bellyache?"

"For *this*." Travis reached under the bed. His hand came back up holding a can of spray paint. Red.

"I found this behind your computer, Darren. I can't believe you would do that to me. Un-freaking-believable."

The floor seemed to drop away beneath me as I stared at the long slim canister. *How could I have been so stupid as to keep that thing?*

"Wait! Let me explain!"

Travis jumped to his feet and loomed over me. "Explain what? That you spray-painted Surfer Dude on that bathroom door? That you set me up? For a month of detention? That you lied to me? Stabbed me in the back? Screwed me over royally?"

"Waldo *made* me do it! He wanted a spy in detention, and I couldn't be the one. It would never have worked!"

"Waldo? *Waldo*??? No, Darren. *You* did this." His finger jabbed me in the chest. "To me. So screw you. This 'friendship'—isn't that a joke—is over."

He tossed the can of paint at me. Instinctively, my hands went up and I caught it. Red-handed, so to speak. I sat there, wordless, holding the incriminating can like it was a nuclear device set to go boom.

My pinkeyed eye began to sting like mad. The not-pinkeyed eye too.

Travis brushed past me, then reconsidered and stopped. He bent over so his mouth was right at my ear.

"And another thing," he said, his breath hot and harsh. "This means war. When I'm through with you, you'll wish Waldo was still your worst enemy."

Creep…creep…creep.

Silent as a mouse, but much more deadly. For I am a ninja, trained in the art of silent approach. In remaining unseen in plain sight.

Unseen, unnoticed, unremarked, overlooked.

Discounted, dismissed.

Discarded.

Dissed.

My dismal reputation does not bother me. In fact, I revel in my very dullness. For dullness is, in reality, the keenest weapon in my ninjan arsenal. After all, attracting attention in Preston Middle, this Arena of Antipathy, remains the surest route to defeat. One for which the only remedy, for a true ninja, is hara-kiri. Suicide.

But today was *not* a good day to die. In fact, it was a perfect day to perform my mission. I had no "ally" alongside me to betray me. I was abandoned, forgotten—on my own.

Excellent.

So I donned my ninja cloak of invisibility. And crept closer, ever closer, to my target. Unseen. Unnoticed. Overlooked. Just the way I like it.

There—my prey. Naturally, she was completely unaware that her doom loomed. Clueless. But she was not innocent. No, no, no—she was certainly not innocent.

Left foot, right foot. Left foot, right foot, I crept. Closer, ever closer.

I ignored all distractions (a shout of "heads up!"—an errant ball bouncing across my path). Nothing could break my focus.

And then—

I pounced.

"Boo."

Startled, she made a little gasp. An *Archie Digest* plummeted into the dirt at her feet. I bent over. Picked it up. I handed it to her, then wrapped my fingers nonchalantly around the swing's chain.

"Oh. Hi, Darren," she said absently. She flipped through the book, trying to regain her page. She obviously didn't think of me as a threat.

Was she ever mistaken. Badly mistaken.

But that was how Dirk Daring liked it—his prey lulled into a sense of security, unguarded. Unaware of his true ninja purpose. Until it was too late.

"Can we talk for a sec?" I said, smiling politely. Meekly, even. I was Good Ol' Darren.

Heh.

Heh.

"Sure..."

I went for her throat.

"You're blackmailing Waldo, aren't you?"

A tiny squeak emerged from her lips. Her eyes darted frantically—left, right, left, right.

"What are you talking about?" Her voice came out high, stifled.

So I had been right. It *had* been her laugh I heard through Waldo's phone!

When I spoke again, my own voice was low, sure. Threatening. No more Mr. Nice Guy. No more meek little mouseman. Heh heh heh.

"I know you are blackmailing him. I want to know about what. And why."

She squeaked again and jumped off the swing. Then she quick-stepped away from me.

"You're crazy, Darren." She tossed her hair.

I grabbed her shoulder before she could escape. I squeezed.

"Tell me. Now!"

"Ow! You're hurting me!" She tried to shake off my grip, but it was too strong for her. For I was Dirk Daring, Secret Agent, Aikido Specialist, Ninja.

"Tell me now. Or I'll tell Travis that you still wet your bed!"

"You wouldn't!"

"Would too."

"It's not true!"

"So what?"

Lucinda's chin jutted forward as she considered her options. There really weren't any. Her shoulders dropped.

A hint of satisfaction, of pride even, crept into her voice. "Fine. What do you want to know?"

"Waldo's secret. What is it?"

"He's been cheating on his math tests."

My mind reeled. It was so unexpected. So unbelievable. I had to probe deeper. Get the real goods.

So I laughed at her. Hoping to wound her pride enough to pry the truth loose.

Lucinda shook her head briskly. "It's true. He's been at it all fall. Buying last year's tests."

"Oh yeah? From who, then?"

"No clue. But I caught him going over them. In a booth at Bo Diddley. I just happened to be there and... well, let's just say you're not the only one with good spy skills, D."

She got a hard, bright look in her eyes. She was telling the truth, I was certain. She was far too smug to be lying. Dirk Daring, Secret Agent/Ninja, could sniff out a liar from fifty paces.

I grabbed the swing's chain again, this time to steady myself. Because Lucinda's story was shocking, if it was true. Shocking—and cataclysmic.

But no—I could not let it rock me. I had to be strong. I had to steel myself to think and to absorb the implications of what I'd just heard.

If Waldo were caught cheating on exams, he could be expelled from school. *Certainly* he'd be stripped of his school presidency.

Lucinda, it seemed, had stumbled upon Waldo dynamite.

Trying not to let the hope, the excitement, color my tone and thereby reveal my secret glee, I probed further.

"Do you have any proof?"

Lucinda shook her head again. "No. I'm pretty sure he's destroyed the old tests. Just my word against his. But I could still make his life pretty miserable. And he knows it."

The strangest look crossed her face. At first I wasn't sure what it meant, but then it clicked.

Lucinda was loving this—all of it. The power. The mind games. *Her* hand on the puppet strings.

Our eyes met, and I saw something new there. Something I recognized.

A half smile played across her lips, and she nodded at me.

Yes, she too was ninja. Unnoticed. Overlooked. Middle School Mulch.

So we understood each other, then.

But I could not be distracted by this newest revelation. It was irrelevant to my purpose. I still had hard information to collect.

"So what did you ask him to do for you?"

She rolled her eyes. "Jeez, Darren. You can be so thick sometimes."

"Just tell me," I said through gritted teeth.

"Isn't it obvious? I told him to keep you away from Travis."

I gawked at her. "Whatttt??? Why on earth would you do that?"

She rolled her eyes again. "Do I have to spell it out for you?"

"Apparently so. Spill. And spell."

I knew she considered chuckling, but one look at my darkened brow and the giggles died in her throat. Instead, she just sighed. "You know how I feel about Travis."

Now it was my turn to roll my eyes.

"Well, you're always *there!* Darren! I can never get any time with him! It's always you butting in, involving him in your stupid schemes. Getting in the way! If you weren't around him so much, I'd have him to myself. And then maybe he'd see…"

Her eyes glistened. Were those actually tears beading in the corners? She turned her face away before I could be sure.

I almost—*almost*—felt sorry for her. Because, of course, she had no chance. Travis couldn't give two hoots about Lucinda. No matter how much time she spent with him, he'd always think she was a freaky, puzzle-loving, loud laugher with about as much charm as a molting hyena.

But you had to admire her cunning. Her determination. They were Superior Spy Skills. Ones *I* could employ.

For my own purposes, of course.

The enemy agent was in his cell. Engaged, no doubt, in the mindless rituals of those in solitary confinement.

Scratching.

Picking.

I did not begrudge my ancient foe these small, physical pleasures. For his last few precious moments of "before" were quickly drawing to an end. The hour had now arrived for me to conduct the interview, as we in the spy trade euphemistically call it. To force his confession of his dark deeds.

The poor fool was as yet unaware of the persuasive powers I would be bringing to my task. The psychological "rack." The emotional "thumb screws." For in the art of mental torture, I was highly skilled. I was the Inquisitor. Torquemada. Saw.

Once I was finished with him, it would always be "after." *After* he had crumbled, unable to withstand my impeccable technique. *After* he had begged for mercy on his knees…

How I looked forward to this—to cracking him like a hazelnut between my remorseless fingers. Wringing the truth from him like dirty water from a string mop. Making him sing.

There would be no mercy, of course. Not from Dirk Daring, Secret Agent. For the tables had turned. The balance shifted.

And now I, Dirk Daring, had the upper hand.

I burst into his room. Closed his bedroom door behind me. Let a glimmer of a smile dance devilishly across my lips.

"To what do I owe this unexpected visit, little bro?"

"I thought we'd play a little game of Truth or Dare tonight."

He laughed. "Sorry, kiddo. I got studying to do. Maybe next time."

I stepped closer to him.

"*Au contraire, mon frère.* I think we'll play now."

Waldo gave me an amused look. One that said, "I'll humor the little twerp." He put down his pen.

"Fine. What's your dare then?"

I shook my head. "No—we're playing truth this time. For the first time. So let's have it."

His brows knit. The corners of his mouth curled down. "If you've got something to say to me, say it. Otherwise, I've got work to do."

"I know about the math tests, *bro.*"

His face grew still.

"I know you bought them. And that Lucinda has been blackmailing you. I know she told you to keep me away from Travis."

Waldo's eyes were hard and cold for a moment, but then he looked away. "Okay. You got me."

"So it is true…"

"It was only that once—I swear! And it was totally unnecessary too. I didn't even need those stupid old exams—I knew the stuff cold. It was just that…with Dad on my case about my marks…well, I felt a little insurance was in order. So in a moment of weakness…"

His eyes landed back on mine. "You won't tell, will you, bro?" I noted his new, pleading tone with pleasure.

I mocked him. Played with him the way a cat torments a mouse. "Who, me? Reveal a secret? Whoa ho ho, oh no…not when it's as good as gold to me. And this is solid gold, my friend. Solid, mathematical gold."

My eyes narrowed. "You know what I want, of course."

"Aw, come on. *You're* not going to blackmail me too, are you? We're *brothers*."

I had to suppress a laugh at that. It wasn't easy, but I did it. I simply smiled at him. Examined my nails. Hummed a little.

Waldo's shoulders sagged even further. "So what do you want then?"

"My journal back."

He gaped at me. "I gave that back to you weeks ago, dude!"

"The copy. Come on, give it back."

"There is no copy, Darren. I never made one. I was just yanking your chain."

Now I gaped at him. "You didn't keep a copy?"

"Naaah…I was just messing with ya. Having a little fun. I'd never tell people about your journal. We're brothers. That would be, well, beyond low."

My knees went weak. I sank to the bed.

I was safe. I'd been safe all along.

"So you won't tell my dad? About buying the test?"

"Not so fast, Waldo. Why did you agree to keep me away from Travis? You know he's my best friend."

My only friend.

"Hey—that was easy. I know you think the world of him, bro, but Travis Sendak is a tool. You really need some space from him."

Anger flared in me like an exploding letter bomb. "You don't know anything about Travis, man! He's been a great friend for, like, ever!"

Waldo shook his head.

"Clueless, clueless, clueless."

"Oh yeah? Well, clue you, Waldo."

I charged for the door.

"I bought them from him, you know."

My hand froze on the doorknob. The back of my neck felt strangely hot. A line of sweat broke out on my upper lip.

I asked Waldo to repeat what he'd said. Unnecessarily, because my gut already knew the truth.

"Those math tests? It was your 'good buddy' Travis who sold them to me. He's the real snake in the grass around here."

I lay on my bed. Unable to move. Unable to think.

Could it really be true?

I remembered Opal saying, *You know you shouldn't trust this guy, right? He's not exactly straight up with you.*

And now this ugly tidbit: Travis was selling math tests.

What else was "my pal" Travis doing that I didn't know about?

Travis was a guy I thought I knew better than myself. But clearly, I didn't know diddly. Not anymore, anyway. The days when we could read each other's minds were long gone.

So maybe it was just as well that Travis wasn't speaking to me. Now that I knew the truth about him, *I* wasn't speaking to *him* either.

After all, a lying, cheating, double-dealing, secret-keeping betrayer was not exactly my idea of a friend.

The playground. Morning recess.

We stood together under the bare branches of the big oak tree, a study in symmetry. Both of us had our hands jammed deep in our pockets. Both of us stared at the toes of our boots.

But it was me who called this meeting. And it was up to me to speak first.

"I know the truth now. What he's been up to," I finally managed to choke out.

Opal looked sad. "I'm really, really sorry, Darren. I didn't want to be the one to have to tell you."

"Well, you're in the clear on that." I had never noticed that smudge of dried dirt on my boot before. I should probably wipe it off. Sometime.

I could hear Opal release her breath in a long, shuddery gasp. Funny, I hadn't realized she'd been holding it. "It's better that you know though. I mean—"

"Yeah. Probably."

"'Cause here he is, going behind your back, laughing at you, showing people your secret book—"

I must have gone white as a marshmallow, because Opal bit her lip and touched my sleeve. "You okay?"

No, I wasn't okay. Opal's revelation had hit me like a swift jab to the intestinal fortitude.

I felt naked. Exposed. Hot and cold, all at once.

Was it really true? In addition to selling tests, had Travis been showing people my journal?

Dear Brother Waldo's words echoed in my head.

BEYOND LOW (low low low looooo…).

"Who?" I asked tonelessly.

"Aw jeez, Darren! I'm sorry! You said you—"

"WHO?"

"Not a lot of people. Just some of the guys. Henry. Vero. Louie."

My gut twisted. One pretzel knot for each name.

How could I ever face those guys again? How, if they knew my secret alter ego's identity? If they knew the real me?

I stumbled away, ducking behind the tree. Let myself sink to the hard, dry dirt there. Let my head fall to my knees.

I began considering all the ways I knew of committing hara-kiri.

The knife to the belly.

The cyanide pill, crushed between the teeth.

The swan dive off a train trestle.

None were adequate—mostly because I couldn't perform any of them right this instant. All I could do was sit there, with my back against the old oak's trunk, and let the horror wash over me.

Endless, endless waves of misery.

Opal came around to my side of the tree. Her eyes were huge, her voice high and shaky.

"Darren! You said you knew!"

No, she hadn't sandbagged me. *I* had sandbagged *her*.

Another wave of horror struck me.

If Opal knew about my journal, she knew what was in it too.

Opal, only the prettiest girl in Preston Middle School. The girl I—

Oh God.

And here she was, right now, staring right into my face.

The shame! The mortification!

If I could have shriveled up and died, I would have. Right there on the spot. But Opal wouldn't let me. She had hunkered down in front of me, and her bright baby blues were fixed on me like surgical lasers. That hard blue gaze wouldn't let me go. It wouldn't let me hide.

I mumbled something, anything, to get her to go. But she wouldn't.

"I'm sorry." Her face and tone were completely sympathetic. It was an even worse form of torture than if she'd flat-out laughed. "So so so so soooooo sorry.

But you said you knew…of course I didn't think there could be anything else besides…but I guess there is."

Her lips tightened into a firm, white line. "So what *did* you know, Darren? If you didn't know about the book? Tell me. Now."

I could not avoid her probing gaze. Could not resist her insistent questioning.

"He was selling tests. To Waldo," I mumbled.

She sank down in the dirt beside me. Ran her hands through her gossamer hair.

"Whoa. That's serious." She snaked her arm around my shoulder. I knew I should have shaken it off, but I was incapable of action. I felt gutted, empty. Done.

Even so, words tumbled from my lips, like someone else was speaking them. They came pouring out of me in great, gasping gulps.

"Something's happened to him. The Travis I know wouldn't do those things. Either of them!"

Opal squeezed my shoulder. I knew I should make her stop, but I didn't. I couldn't.

Her face grew thoughtful. "Yeah. I hear you. He was always kind of a jerk. But he was never evil. And he's turned evil now, hasn't he?"

I couldn't answer her. My throat had gone tight. Thick. I quickly wiped my eyes with the back of my hand—it wouldn't do to let Opal see me cry.

It wouldn't do at all.

I could feel Opal thinking, hard, beside me.

"The question is, why? What happened to Travis that would make him do what he's been doing? 'Cause you're right—it's not like him. Not at all."

Her face brightened. She punched me lightly in the arm. "So this is good news!"

"Sure. Right."

She punched me in the arm again, harder this time.

"Don't be such a poophead. Look at the upside! There are mysteries to solve! Secrets to de-secret! In fact, this sounds like the perfect mission for a guy I know. Dirk Daring. Ever heard of him?"

I have agreed to work with a new, untried partner on this most dangerous, most critical of missions. To do so is not the normal practice of secret agents at my level of accomplishment and responsibility. Especially once our cover has been blown. But flexibility is the hallmark of the master spy. When Opportunity knocks, one opens the door and grabs her by the hand. And there is none more flexible, or grabalacious, than Dirk Daring, Secret Agent.

I cannot risk entering the Dragon's Den. So at Mission Go! Hour 0:00:00, I lurked in the shadows that shrouded the water fountain. Looking left, right.

Making sure no one saw Agent Jewel and me together. Our success depended upon our discretion.

All clear. I gave the go signal to Agent Jewel. On my mark, she disappeared into the cafeteria. The Dragon's Den.

There, on the Inside, she would be my eyes. There, on the Inside, she would be my ears. She would stalk the dragon in his lair and learn his secrets.

I waited.

Left, right. Left, right. Nothing.

Patiently, I waited.

One minute. Two minutes. Three minutes.

Could I trust her spycraft? Her talent for observing unobserved? I confess, I was completely outside my comfort zone. For even Dirk Daring, Secret Agent, has vulnerabilities. Even he can be undone.

Suddenly, she was at my side.

"Dang! How do you do that?" I said, trying to still my rapid-fire heart.

She smirked, just a tad. "Do what?"

"Forget it. Report, Agent Jewel."

"Yes sir, captain sir!" She snapped her heels together and gave me a mock salute.

I glared at her.

"Oh for crying out loud, Darren. Lighten up."

"Report."

"All right, all right. It's just like you said would happen. With you sidelined, Lu has got Travis cornered. Practically has him in a headlock. If I wasn't hating him so much, I'd feel sorry for him."

"There is no place for emotion in the shadow world," I reminded her.

Was that laughter rippling across her lips? No—for Agent Jewel was a professional. She would not laugh in the face of duty. Only in the face of danger.

"Right. I'll do another pass in"—she checked her gadgety, oversized watch—"35 seconds."

We stood side by side, waiting while her praise-worthy timepiece ticked away the seconds.

"This is fun," Agent Jewel said. "Being on a mission."

Dare I admit that her radiant smile struck me down, leaving me defenseless?

I swallowed hard. Shook the feeling off. It was dangerous to allow myself to be unmanned so. The shadow world, after all, is no place for emotion.

I pointed at the cafeteria doors. "3...2...1...go."

She gave me another mock salute and slipped away.

I waited.

One minute.

Two minutes.

Three minutes.

A burst of sound—laughter, the clatter of trays— as Opal came flying through the doors. Face flushed. Breathing hard.

"We got a problem, D."

I held my finger to my lips. Motioned her to accompany me to the library. Where we could talk privately.

Quickly, quietly, we made our way through the empty corridors. When we were finally ensconced in a study carrel, we bent our heads together. Colleagues. Conspirators. Collaborators.

"What happened?" I whispered.

"Lucinda—she's O.P."

"O.P.?"

"Out of the picture. She wasn't sitting with Travis anymore. I couldn't find her at first. Finally, I spotted her. She was sulking over a grilled cheese sandwich. At the loner table by the window."

"So he gave her the heave-ho. As predicted." I gave myself a mental check mark in the "correct" column.

"And T-Bone? What was he doing?"

Opal bit her lip. "He was up to no good. We're in big trouble, dude."

My blood froze in my veins as I pictured Travis flaunting my spy journal, showing it off to everyone he could. Pointing out the "good parts." *The most embarrassing parts.* I could practically hear the mocking laughter ringing in my ears.

How could I have been so stupid? Handing him the very keys to my humiliation?

Easy—I'd thought he was my friend.

"Go ahead. I can take it. Tell me." My voice sounded flat even to my own ears.

"He was with Amber! They were, like, together!!! Heads practically touching! Laughing and giggling. They were whispering together like...like..." She stared into my eyes. "Well, like us!"

"Colluding with the enemy," I said, staring right back. Man, her eyes were blue.

"Consorting," she replied breathlessly.

"This can't be good," I said.

"No. It can't," she said.

The next time we met, it was in the War Room.

Opal surveyed the space with critical detachment.

"Nice digs, D." She pointed at the poster over the bed. "Didn't take you for a *Star Wars* fan though."

"Yeah, well. We put that up when I was, like, 6. Never got around to taking it down."

She spread her arms wide. "Well, maybe you should call this the Wars Room, then. Hey—don't get mad! I'm joking. *Joking!!* Your room's nice. Really."

She glanced around again, her head nodding appreciatively. Her fingers hopscotched through the jumble on my dresser. "You sure have a lot of computer stuff in here."

"Hey! Don't touch that! It's delicate."

"What is it?"

"A motion detector." I took it out of her hands. "It sounds an alarm whenever anyone unauthorized comes into my room. It doesn't work though—the batteries are dead."

"*Hnph*. That's too bad. I coulda used one of those to keep Amber out. Except we shared a room, ha ha. What's this?"

"Come on! Leave my stuff alone!"

"What is it?" she said again, fingering the LEDS and levers on the console.

"It's a lie-detector set. Put it down, okay?"

"Okay! Okay!" She replaced the kit exactly as she had found it, lining it up just so, letting her hand linger a tad longer than necessary on its shiny black cover. "I sure wish I had one of these..."

Her index finger trailed across it one more time. Then Opal crossed her arms and squared her shoulders. "So. What's the plan here?"

I got down on my hands and knees and pulled a stack of plywood sheets out from under my desk. I lifted off the top sheet and selected the uppermost map—one I'd drawn up earlier in the week.

I cleared a space on my desk and laid the map—it was more of a chart, actually—out flat.

"Wow," Opal said, "that's pretty cool too. Great job on the lettering. Love how you did that 3D thing."

"Thanks." I gave her a curt nod. "Now, let me explain what's what. Here are the battle lines. As of last week."

"Is that me?" Opal pointed to the sparkly diamond I'd penciled in under *Green Team*.

I cleared my throat and decided to sidestep her seriously embarrassing question. I dove into my desk drawer, searching for my extremely-hard-to-find cupcake eraser.

When I judged it was safe to surface, I began vigorously cupcaking names and lines off the map.

"Right. So this is the original survey map. There've been some major changes, though, since I made it."

I grabbed some colored pencils and quickly roughed in all the current alliances and positions.

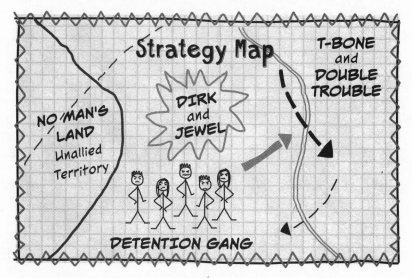

"You'll notice this new version is missing a few key combatants. That's because they're loose cannons right now—unallied forces we can't be sure of."

I picked an old plastic Smurf guy out of the jumble on my desk. He was holding a champagne bottle that read *Happy Smurfday*. "This one's Waldo."

Then I grabbed a pad of Post-its and quickly drew a goony face on it. "This one's Lucinda."

I placed the Smurf and the Post-it pad on the board in No Man's Land/Unallied Territory.

"Yeah. I see why you don't want to draw them in yet," Opal said. "You can't be sure where they stand."

"Exactly. Take Lucinda, for instance." I tapped on the Post-it pad. "She was definitely Team Travis, and therefore on my team, when I drew up the first battle plan—100 percent all the way." I pushed the pad into the Travis-controlled zone. "But now that we're splits, and Amber's moved in on Travis territory..."

Opal nudged the Post-it pad right off the map. "She's out."

"You sure?"

"Oh yeah. 'Hell hath no fury like a woman scorned.' And Lucinda is definitely a woman scorned. You shoulda seen her face Friday in the lunchroom..." Opal nodded decisively. "Trust me on this—Lucinda can be turned. Give me five minutes with her and she'll be working for us."

She picked up the Post-it pad and dropped it into our zone. *Plunk.* "Meet Agent Fury. Team Us."

A queasy feeling turned in my gut. "I dunno. Remember, she threw me under a bus..."

Opal waved away my objection.

"Forget it. She wasn't thinking about you. She would have thrown her own mother under if she thought it would get her with Travis. Don't know what she sees in him, actually, but hey, no accounting for taste, is there?" She smiled, just a tiny bit, then flicked her blond hair behind her shoulder. "Agent Fury—yeah, I really like the sound of that. She'd have to be Junior Agent Fury, of course. Following my orders."

She picked up the Smurf and twirled it in her fingers. "But what about him? Where does Waldo fit now that you know about the book and the tests and everything?"

"Why don't you ask him yourself?" came a voice through the wall.

"ARE YOU EAVESDROPPING ON US, YOU... YOU...SNEAK?" I shouted.

Waldo appeared in the doorway. "Dude, haven't you noticed? The walls in this house are like rice paper. I can hear you fart in your sleep. So no, I wasn't 'spying' on you. God forbid, 'cause spying is wrong, eh?" He chuckled to himself. "But I did hear someone call 'my name.'" He made air quotes with his fingers. "Wallllll-do. Hey— maybe that's why I can hear through walls. Walls are my"—more air quotes—"'secret power.' Wall-do. Get it?"

Opal tightened her arms over her chest. "So. Whose side are you on in this? Other than your own, of course."

Waldo shook his head mournfully. "So young, so jaded." He flung himself onto my bed. Acting all Lord and Master-y. "Look, I'm not really into your silly spy games. But I already told you, I think Travis is a douche. I didn't like him from the first day I slapped an eyeball on him."

"More like since the first day you realized he'd got you by the short hairs," I said.

"Knowing about how you're a cheater and all," Opal said.

Waldo shook his head. "Naaah—he can't do a thing. If he outs me, he outs himself too, right? But here's what *I* want to know."

He stretched himself out on my bed, resting his head in his clasped hands. I cringed, knowing where those hands might have been recently.

"We got that boy a month in detention, right?"

Opal and I both nodded.

"My idea was he'd report back to you on what was going on up there, right? Find out what those guys were talking about. Maybe get some dirt on who was organizing the whole school bus-lunch money-shake-down gig."

"He was only up there because you tricked me into—"

Waldo held up one hand. "Focus, little bro, focus. He was there, okay? Who cares why. He was on the inside track to get the goods. But what did he report? Nothin'."

I crossed my arms. "He said nobody talked. Because Miss Robinette was practically *Der Führer.*"

Waldo abruptly leaned toward us. His dark eyes intense. Bullets.

"That's pure, unadulterated BS."

"Which, of course, you'd know all about," said Opal.

Waldo gave her a sharp look and replied in a sing-songy voice, "No, it's not something I know all about,

Miss Priss. But Miss Robinette is my English teacher. And she's no dragon. She's *hot*."

"Ugh," Opal said.

"Yeah, well, ugh you, okay? She's super nice too. So no, she doesn't make those detention goons keep quiet. They're keeping mum for some other reason."

"Or Travis lied. About what they were talking about," I said.

"Exactamundo. Because he didn't want to clue you in. Now as school president, it is my business to know what's going on at Preston. Everything, including what those naughty detention boys are up to. That's why I wanted you to get Travis into detention in the first place, right?"

"You killed two birds with one stone..." I said, getting it at last.

"You hear that?" He cupped his ear with his hand. "That's the other shoe dropping. *Mazel tov.* So here's the deal, little bro. I'm on your side on this one. Because I want you to find out what Travis is up to with those detention losers. And the best way to do that is for you to get yourself into detention too."

"No way!"

"He's right," Opal said.

"Oh great, now you're on his side too?"

"I'm on the side of making life at school bearable. And if finding out why Travis is acting like such a colossal you-know-what is the way to do that, then finding out what he knows about the Detention Gang might be part of the solution. Not to mention, D, you've got to figure out how to get your book back."

Waldo shook his head and laughed. "That stupid book, man. *Mind-Blowing Missions*. How freaking lame is that?"

It was Opal who hauled off and chucked the motion detector at him. Hit him square in the eye too.

Transcript of phone call by Mrs. Helen Troy to Preston Middle School's school secretary. 96700001111ZZZA De-encrypted. 11/23 08:33.

Hi, Val. This is Helen Troy calling. Jason Arsenico's stepmom. He's in Miss Robinette's homeroom class, Room 22? Yeah, I think that's the number. Anyway, Jason won't be in today. He got hit in the eye yesterday. With a softball, I think. It's swollen shut. Yeah, it's pretty bad. No, I'm sure his vision will be fine once the swelling comes down. But we'll keep him home today. Thanks, Valerie. Talk to you soon.

As soon as I entered my classroom, I discovered the new phase of hostilities had already begun.

There, on my desk, was a page from my journal. A very sharp pencil had been shoved through it, pinning it to the wood underneath.

As kids came in, they sidled over to look. Henry. Louie.

They tittered. Glanced at me and quickly glanced away. Tittered again.

Travis, meanwhile, just sat at his desk like a king. Cracking his knuckles. *Poppity pop. Poppity pop pop.*

I yanked the pencil out of the desktop. Folded the skewered journal page neatly. Stuck it in my back pocket. And then I sat at my desk, running my finger back and forth, back and forth, over the new hole there.

If Miss Templeton saw it, I'd be getting a detention for sure. Even though I'd had nothing to do with it. 'Course, I'd never snitch—that would be like announcing to the world, "I am a weenie, unable to handle my own problems." I'd be asking for punishment.

A *well-deserved* punishment.

I considered my options. Gauged the strength of my forces. Analyzed my position.

And opted for all-out attack.

I carefully scanned the ground. Left, right, left, right. Nothing.

The bare earth was just that—bare. Of course, this field had been cleared of mines—the red No Dogs Allowed sign attested to its pure state.

But this is the shadow world, where nothing exists in its idealized form. This is the dark side, where the forbidden is done under cover and in stealth.

Hence I did not give up hope. Patience, after all, is the trademark quality of Dirk Daring, Secret Agent.

He who is patient will succeed.

He who searcheth will findeth.

And findeth I do, pardon the pun. A perfect specimen. It was practically still steaming in the wintry air. Sending up its signature scent like a homage to venality.

I removed the sheet of cardboard I had secreted in my inside coat pocket. Carefully, oh so carefully, I slid my treasure, my "diamonds," onto the cardboard, pushing them ever so gently with a twig.

Carefully, oh so carefully, I carried my treasure to the north doors. Left, right, left, right I peered—no one was watching. Quick as a jackrabbit, I hopped to. Slipped between the doors. Hugged the wall, hoping no one would pass by, no one would notice me with my "grenade."

I slipped onto the battlefield. All was quiet. The enemy had foolishly abandoned the field, attending to his daily needs. But I, Dirk Daring, have no needs other than victory.

I moved quickly but silently to the enemy's field unit HQ. Slipped the cardboard, with its poodley payload, into place in the interior of his desk. Arranged it just so, for maximum hand-to-turd contact.

Then I turned tail and ran, escaping unseen, unheard, knowing doggie doom awaited my erstwhile friend, my sworn enemy.

Tick. Tick. Tick.

Who knew 60 minutes could pass so slowly?

Torture. Ultimate torture.

Tick. Tick. Tick.

I surreptitiously studied my companions on Cell Block D.

T-Bone, of course. Still smarting from the wounds he'd received in action. I couldn't help but smile as I recalled the fallout from my bomb. The screams. The hooted laughter. The "Stink hand! He's got stink hand!" yells.

And the pats on the back I received. The whispered "good ones" and "nice works."

The sweet taste of victory.

I almost laughed out loud recalling the jokes that flew around the class all day like tracer fire. "*Doo* me a favor, Travis?" "I keep on *dropping* things today—any idea why, Travis?" "Wow, I'm *pooped* today. How about you, Travis?"

But I just kept my head down. I knew hostilities between Travis and me had only just begun.

This would be a long war, a war of attrition. And I had staying power—I had proven that much already. But how much staying power did Travis have? Impossible to know—about this new Travis anyway.

I had expected to hear the low murmur of poo jokes up here in detention too, but no. The Detention Gang didn't mention it. In fact, they seemed strangely quiet, much like Travis had described them.

Had he been telling the truth about that? Or was there another reason for their silence?

Perhaps on Cell Block D, holding your tongue was the way it was done. You just put in your time, counting down the minutes of your sentence. Tick. Tick. Tick. 38. 37. 36.

I had four more days to find out. Four more days in detention, along with my archenemy, Travis Sendak, and the goons of Cell Block D.

The next morning dawned clear and bright. I knew it would hold…something.

But what? I knew Travis would launch a counterattack. But I had no idea what it would be.

I'd spent the entire night tossing and turning, considering the possibilities. They were legion. No way could I prepare for each and every one.

I'd just have to be on guard, yet adaptable. Ready to respond, as appropriate, no matter where the action happened. I'd need all my Dirk Daring skills for sure.

When I opened my front door, Opal was there.

"Jeez! You gotta stop appearing out of the blue like that! You scared the crap out of me!" My voice sounded embarrassingly like a girl's.

"Sorry," Opal said, *her* voice sounding just fine. She was grinning ear to ear behind her scarf. "I just figured you'd be better off this morning if you weren't on your own. In case of an ambush. Amber's good at that."

"So are you."

"Maybe, but not as good as Amber."

We walked toward school together, companionably, our feet hitting the pavement in unison. I counted in my head how many steps before we fell out of sync—42.

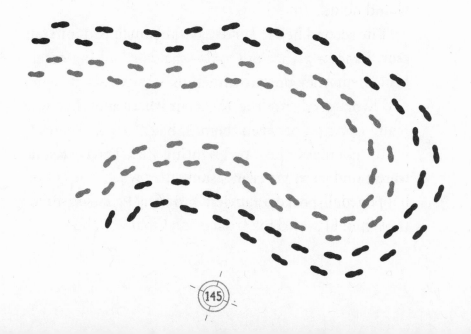

I knew we were both thinking the same thing. Would Travis snooker me? Would Amber attack Opal? No telling. At least we had each other's backs.

We made it into school, and to our lockers, without incident. We didn't even see Travis or Amber.

The first bell rang. Opal and I gave each other a thumbs-up for support and headed into Room 5. Travis was already there. At his desk, seemingly finishing up some homework.

Yeah right.

I checked my seat carefully before I sat down. My desk too. Top. Bottom. Sides.

All clear.

The second bell rang just as Amber slipped into her seat. I shot a glance at Opal—she was looking determinedly in the opposite direction.

I wondered, for the thousandth time, what was really going on between them. It had to suck, whatever it was. No matter how bad fighting with Travis was, he wasn't my sister. My twin sister.

The loudspeaker crackled into life. "Please stand for the national anthem."

We stood. Shifted from foot to foot as the tinny music played.

With half an ear, I listened to the morning announcements.

"Good morning. I'm Yasmin…and I'm Bree… with your Preston morning report. Today is Tuesday, November 24. There will be a meeting of the yearbook committee in the multipurpose room during second lunch period. All students are welcome. There will be practice for the badminton team in the north gym, also during second lunch period. Intramural indoor soccer will continue in the south gym during both lunch periods. Today's matches are between the Puddlejumpers and the Wannabes, first lunch, and Arsenal and Sockitwrench, second lunch. Come out and support your favorite team."

Yasmin whoever-she-was rustled some papers.

"And now we have a special announcement. From Dirk Daring."

My gut flip-flopped. My ears, my throat and my heart went cold.

"*The alley was narrow,*" Yasmin read. "*Dark and narrow. It stank like rotted vegetables and cat pee, the signature reek of demoralization and despair. I flattened myself like a tortilla against the bricks. I had just one task now—to melt into the wall. To become the wall...The forces of darkness were on the move...And they were hunting for me. Dirk Daring, Secret Agent."*

I forced myself to raise my eyes to Travis. A nasty grin distorted his mouth.

A Joker smile.

I leapt from my seat. Threw myself across the room. Grabbed Travis by the throat and wrestled him out of his chair.

"You'll pay for this!" I shouted in his face. And then—

Well, I don't know exactly what happened next. I was pummeling him, hitting him as hard as I could, while inside my head, red, purple and black spangles of rage exploded. I was crying and screaming, hitting and kicking at him as he hit me back. Then other people's hands were on us, clutching, pulling us away from each other, but without success. I just kept hitting and kicking him, each punch feeling like it had been building up in me for years. Now it was rocketing out like puke when you've got the flu. You feel awful, but relieved at the same time.

And then we were both being force-marched down to Principal Bonaparte's office.

The End.

✿ ✿ ✿

Only it wasn't the end.

There was the long awful hour in the office, sitting side by side with Travis. Not speaking. Not looking at each other. Every fiber of us vibrating with rage.

And then there was the lecture. And the news.

Suspension.

Three days.

For fighting.

Now it was

The. End.

Notes from Suspended Animation.
12X12144CODZZZ De-encrypted. 11/25.

I have been grounded in addition to being suspended.

No telephone. No computer. No TV.

I am forced to remain in my room except for meals. Solitary confinement.

I have nothing to do but read over the few entries I had wisely held back from my journal binder and hidden in Confidential Location #34 *For My Eyes Only.* Thank God not all is revealed.

Besides that, I have nothing else to do but write my thoughts out. Here. In slow, neat longhand.

So I write. For posterity. For distraction.

Curly-tailed *y*'s. Neatly crossed *t*'s.

But nothing can distract me truly. Not from the terrible thoughts that circle like vultures in my head.

For this suspension is not my true punishment. Not my true torture. The true torture is knowing that while I sit here, immobilized, Preston Middle School is reading my journal. Every last (binderized) word of it. They have heard the earliest entry, my soul's secrets blaring out through the school loudspeakers. No doubt additional entries are now being passed hand to hand, courtesy of Amber. Double Trouble.

How I had underestimated my foes. They were more evil, even, than Waldo. More mercenary. More ruthless.

Because Waldo, as it turned out, had some ruth. He had declined to make my journal public, admitting that doing so would be lower than ant belly.

At dinner tonight, Waldo shot me sympathetic glances. I ignored them. They were too painful to me. Sympathy from Waldo! I'd just as soon stick pins in my eyes than accept that ignoble offering.

I knew I could ask Waldo what was happening at school and he would tell me the truth. The truth—ha! A concept I never would have associated with Brother Waldo before.

But the real truth was this: I couldn't bear to learn the truth. Imagining the worst was not as bad as *knowing* the worst. I would not be able to stand having my fears confirmed.

Yes, it's true. Even master spies can be broken.

Better, much better, to hover somewhere in the shadow world of denial. A place I had grown to love.

This state of suspended animation will not last, of course.

When my suspension period is over, I'll have to walk the long, last walk into Preston, accompanied by the jeers and taunts of my detractors.

They'll enjoy seeing Dirk Daring swing. They'll yank down on my legs even.

If only the end will be merciful.

If only it will be quick.

Yeah. Right.

Black Monday. My first day back to school, and Opal was not waiting for me at my front door.

That told me everything I needed to know. My humiliation at school was so complete, Opal could no longer risk being associated with me. Her own cool factor would be too compromised. For the taint of social outcastry, there is no cure. Once acquired, it cannot be lost.

I understood that.

I respected that.

I knew how the game was played at Preston Middle School. Had I not been playing it myself for two whole years? But now it was time to own up. To man up.

To admit the Truth. With a bold, capital, flat-topped, longhand *T*.

Yes, it is true—I, Darren Dirkowitz, am also Dirk Daring.

Go ahead—laugh if you want.

I am who I am. Take it or leave it.

I walked alone toward my doom, knowing the kids at school were all going to choose "leave."

The sad Truth was, I wasn't too popular before.

I probably wouldn't notice much difference now.

I lurked on the street corner near the school until the last possible second. If I was lucky, I could just make it to my locker and into class as the second bell sounded. I'd be able to put off the inevitable mockery till morning recess at least.

BBBBRRRRRIIIINNNNNGGGG!!!!

I ran. Judging my moment perfectly (thank those Dirk Daring reflexes, ha ha), I reached the north doors just as the hallways began to empty.

Locker.

Lock.

Door.

Seat.

BBBBRRRRRIIIINNNNNGGGG!!!!

Whew. Safe.

Naturally, everyone stared at me.

I dared them with my eyes: *Go ahead—flush me.*

So why were they smiling? Why were they giving me ups?

I'd barely had time to consider the possibilities when the loudspeaker crackled into life. "Please stand for the national anthem."

We stood, as usual. Shifted from foot to foot, as usual, while the tinny music played. I felt my cheeks redden in shame as I remembered the last time I'd done this...and knew everyone else was remembering it too.

Then the anthem ended and we sat for the announcements.

"Good morning. I'm Erik...and I'm Mo...with your Preston morning report. Today is Monday, November 30. We hope everyone enjoyed a wonderful weekend and has come back to school energized for a week of learning. There will be a meeting of the yearbook committee in the multipurpose room during second lunch period. All students are welcome. There will be practice for the badminton team in the north gym, also during second lunch period. Intramural indoor soccer will continue in the south gym during both lunch periods. Today's matches are between the Puddlejumpers and Sockitwrench, first lunch, and Timbits and Gogogo, second lunch. Come out and support your favorite team. There will be a meeting of the Dirk Daring Fan Club during afternoon recess..."

My head snapped around on my neck. My temple pulsed crazily. My mouth went dry.

Left, right, I scanned the room—yes, they were all still staring at me. Nodding. Some even clapped.

What was going on?

An origami crane fluttered onto my desk. Pink.

I unfolded it.

Opal's handwriting, teeny tiny, on the white side.[3]

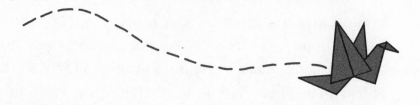

---

3   Code LW1: Read last word first (and keep going).
The note was signed "Love, Agent Jewel, aka Opal." With two fat x's and two fat o's.

"????? Awesome it isn't. Yourself by all stuff great such written you've believe can one no and smart and funny and fun. Hilarious are you thinks everyone. H.E.R.O. Hero a are you now because. Ha ha hardee, them on backfired it but... provided promptly Trouble Double and Travesty which! More for clamoring were they!!! It loved people? Week last speaker -loud the over book your of part that. Phone the to come to allowed weren't you said mom your but, you call to tried I."

Opal came rushing up to me.

"Did you see this? Hot off the press!"

She thrust the Monday edition of the *Preston Prestige* at me. There, on the front page, was an excerpt from *The Mind-Blowing Missions of Dirk Daring, Secret Agent.*

Special to the Preston Prestige!
BY AMBER VEGA, REPORTER

Many Preston students have seen the abridged versions of the suddenly popular book "The Mind-Blowing Missions of Dirk Daring, Secret Agent" floating around the school. Here, for the first time, you can read chapter one in its entirety. STAY TUNED for further chapters in future editions of everyone's favorite school newspaper, the P.P.!

I tried to concentrate on the words. But how could I? Those bleepity bleep bleeps had reprinted my journal, my *private* words, in the school paper! Without my permission! The nerve! The gall! The—

"Incredible reversal, isn't it?" Opal said, jumping up and down with excitement. "This is your big op, Darren! Your chance to shine!"

"I'll make them pay for this..." I said through clenched teeth.

Opal flicked my bicep with one porcelain finger. "Hey—smarten up. Revenge is for losers. And you are the winner here. They printed this as a way to salvage their own reps. Don't you see? You've *got* your revenge!

"Now, here's what we're gonna do—we're gonna maximize. Follow this up with you giving me an exclusive interview with you—the author!"

As Opal spoke, I felt a warm glow suffuse my body. She was right, of course. We could snatch victory out of the jaws of defeat. *And* be magnanimous about it. No reason to grind faces in the dirt. Dirt was their natural element, after all.

Vero Spadifora, dribbling a soccer ball, came running up to me. He smiled and clapped me on the back.

"Your story's awesome, dude. Can't wait to read the next installment!"

He was gone before I could even answer.

"Wow! A drive-by—make that dribble-by—review! Five stars!" Opal hooted, giving me a fist bump.

After that, I was in a bit of a daze. Everywhere I looked, kids were reading the P.P.

Opal patted the swing next to her. "I haven't read the whole thing yet."

"Yeah. Me neither," I said, sitting in it. "I guess I should. This installment that they printed is old—at least a month. I don't really even remember what it said."

"You should probably read it over again, then. Before I interview you anyway. You want to sound as brill as you can. As you are."

I smoothed the newsprint and started reading.

"*The alley was narrow—dark and narrow. It stank like rotted vegetables and cat pee, the signature reek of demoralization and despair...*"

My eyes slid hungrily down the page.

"*There was nothing to see, nothing to fear. Not unless you counted the rats that squeaked behind the Nino's Pizza dumpster...But nothing is as it seems in the* shadow world. I knew the forces of darkness were on the move. Watching, waiting. And they were hunting for me. Dirk Daring, Secret Agent…mistakes are for corpses, not master spies like me."

"Heh," I chuckled. "That's pretty funny. 'Mistakes are for corpses.'"

"Yeah." Opal nodded. She was sucking on a Tootsie Roll Pop as she read. "You really have a way with words."

I kept reading.

"I slid my key silently into the doorknob and placed my hand on the sensor pad—it was cunningly disguised as a plain green shingle. Only once my unique handprint was read and identified would my key be enabled.

"As I waited for clearance, I attuned my highly trained senses to the surroundings. I heard nothing but the wind whispering in the maple trees. The single woof! of a dog let out to do his business.

"I heard the click that meant my clearance had been approved. I entered.

"The next thing I knew, I was on the floor, my arm twisted behind my back. And my archenemy, Allegra Montefiore, was whispering in my ear. 'Tell me where the disc is now, Dirk, or you die.'"

I dropped the paper to my lap. "Hey…what the—!"

"What the what?" Opal mumbled, absorbed in her reading.

"This end bit! About another spy, Allegra something or other. I didn't write that!"

Opal stopped swinging.

"What? Where?" she said.

"The very end. The last line before 'To Be Continued…' I didn't write that!"

Her eyes skipped to the bottom of the page. Left, right, they flicked.

"Oh. My. God." Opal's face was the color of chalk.

"Opal? You okay?"

When she looked back at me, her eyes were blazing. With anger. I thought I saw fear there too.

"It's Amber, of course. She's the one who changed your story! Because it's not enough for her to zing you. She's going to zing me too."

Her face contorted into one of those mask of tragedy thingies.

"That mystery character in your story? Allegra? Allegra Montefiore? That's me! Amber's not just stealing *your* story. She's taking mine too."

"I'm not sure I'm getting this," I said to Opal when we finally had the chance to talk again. "Who is this Allegra Whoever, and what does she have to do with you?"

Opal gave me a look that could send butter right back up into a cow's udders.

"Don't you get it, Darren? You're not the only one who has a fantasy. A dream."

She walked a little ways away from me. I could see her shoulders shaking. Her hands opened and closed, opened and closed, at her sides.

"You're right. I don't get it. Not one bit. Are you telling me you keep a mission journal like I do?"

She shook her head. "But when we were kids, both Amber and I used to play spies. Kim Possible. Power-Puff Girls. You know, stuff like that. We'd dress up and run around and save the planet from evil Dr. Xes. We each had favorite characters we pretended to be. Hers was Candy Kane. I was Allegra Montefiore." She paused, taking a breath.

"Well, she kind of got bored with it. Claimed she'd 'outgrown that stupid stuff.' But I never thought it was stupid. I still like to imagine I'm Allegra every once in a while."

Opal's voice had started to crack as she talked, but now she was crying full-out. "She's doing this to hurt me. To embarrass me. I can't believe she'd be so mean!" she sobbed.

I didn't know what to do. Here she was, the beautiful Opal Vega, her face in her hands, crying so hard it would make even an evil Dr. X's heart break. It was unbearable.

I had to do something. Anything.

So, okay. It wasn't pretty. I kind of even hit her in the chin by accident. But even so, I somehow managed to put my arms around her. I pulled her to me and murmured some nonsense words in her ear, the way my mom used to whisper to me when I'd hurt myself and had run to her for a hug. Opal didn't push me away. In fact, she kinda leaned in closer to me and put her arms around my waist.

"Shh, shh," I said.

"Oh! Oh! Oh!" she sobbed wetly against my shoulder.

I patted her back, feeling foolish as all get-out. But good, too, somehow.

Eventually her sobs turned to sniffles. And then she was turning her head, wiping her eyes and straightening up, leaving me standing apart from her, my arms hanging like shovels at my sides.

She forced a crooked smile and glanced up at me, then away.

Embarrassed.

Well, good—that made two of us.

"Thanks, Darren." She sniffed again.

"It's not so bad," I said. "First of all, no one knows who Allegra Montyhoozy is but you, me and Amber. Maybe Travis. Right?"

"Right…"

"And didn't you just tell me this is a chance to turn ignominy into victory?"

Her forehead crinkled. "Ignomi-hoo?"

"Sorry," I said, feeling dorkier than ever. "I mean humiliation, defeat. Whatever."

She shook her head. "This is different. It's not about them." She tipped her head toward the other kids racing around the schoolyard. "It's about Amber 'n' me."

"What's up between you two anyway? This seems like more than the ordinary, sisterly type of fighting. I don't remember you two ever going at it like this before."

"We never did," she said, wiping her nose. "Not until..."

Her shoulders slumped.

"Not until what?"

"I'm not supposed to tell..."

"Yeah, well, she's not supposed to print your secrets in the school paper, is she? I think you're okay to tell me. I'm good at keeping secrets. Dirk Daring, right?" I pointed to my chest and struck a goofy, superhero stance.

It worked: I got that crooked smile again. It nearly tore my heart in two.

She took a deep breath. A decision-making breath.

"It was when she got the stupid LD designation," Opal finally said. "That's when everything went south."

"LD? As in learning disability?"

Opal nodded. "Yeah. She was having trouble with math. Geometry especially. You know how we have to make shapes on those geoboard things? With the rubber bands? She can't do it. Not at all. Ms. Scribner told our mom she should get Amber tested, and she did, and it turns out that Amber has, like, a gynormous 'deficit' in spatial sense. And working memory too. Apparently she sucks at working memory."

"So what? Everybody sucks at something. Only some people get the paperwork to prove it."

"That's what I thought too, but Amber got all down on herself. And then she got pissed at me. Like it was my fault she had this LD thing and I didn't. And she started being really mean, to everyone really, but especially to me. She's been like some kind of she-wolf since then."

"She-wolf," I said with a chuckle. "Nice one."

The bell rang. We started heading into the building, me still trying to make sense of what Opal was telling me.

"So she's feeling like crap...and that's why she's gotten so mean. But it's all so dumb! I mean,

Amber is plenty smart and pretty and she can do lots of stuff! Who cares about geoboards or working whatever?"

"Amber does, of course. And Travis too."

"Travis?"

"They go to the same tutor now. On Tuesday afternoons."

I stopped in my tracks.

"Travis goes to karate on Tuesday afternoons. He has for years."

Opal snorted. "Oh yeah? Would that be Bright Horizons Learning Center—Specializing in Math, English and Roundhouse Kicks? 'Cause trust me—he goes to Bright Horizons every week. I've seen him there when we pick up Amber. And they're not doing much karate. That's why he and Amber have gotten so tight. They both have a secret. The *same* secret."

Left, right. Left, right.

No one is watching. I creep closer to my access point—the cat door.

"You can really fit through that thing?" Agent Jewel inquired.

"I think the parameters are acceptable. They were in August anyway."

"You've grown some," said Agent Fury. "If you get stuck…"

"I won't get stuck. Getting stuck is for stickers."

We all laughed.

Being on a mission with friends was fun. Even if it was the most serious mission of my life.

It didn't matter that Darren Dirkowitz had become a so-called Hero at school. His deepest, darkest secrets, even if no longer secret, were in the possession of the enemy.

Dirk Daring had been assigned to repatriate them. To bring the binder home.

"You're absolutely sure Travis won't be out of his tutor session until 4:45?" I asked Agent Jewel.

"At the earliest," she said with a curt nod.

"That gives us 15 minutes clear. Plus driving-home time. I don't want to dip into that safety margin. I'll be out in less than 10. Fury, you watch at the front. Signal Jewel if you see the T-Bone mobile approaching. Copy that?"

"Copy." Agent Fury scooted around to the front of the house.

"You got your phone on?" I asked Agent Jewel.

She held it to her lips. "Can you hear me?" The reverb through my own phone nearly blew my eardrums out.

"Okay, I'm going in," I mouthed.

She nodded and mouthed back, "Ten-four."

Travis and I had been using the cat door for getting in and out of his house for, like, ever. It was too small for a grown-up to fit through. But it was just right for Travis's very fat cat, Nibs. And also for a boy with a bad habit of forgetting his house key.

Sure enough, it was unlocked. I ran my finger under the edge and lifted the flap up easily. Now to squirm my way inside…

Agent Jewel held the door open for me. She gave me a quick, bolstering pat on the back. And then I was shimmying through the opening and into Travis's house.

It was a tight squeeze—I *had* grown since the last time I'd done this—but it was still okay. I was in!

I raced for the stairs. Up to Travis's room.

Where would he have stashed my binder?

No problem—it was right there, front and center, in the middle of his desk.

I picked it up and riffled through the pages to make sure they were complete.

They were all there, all right.

But—wait! What the heck was this!????

Anger roared through me like a hot tsunami. *Travis had written all over the pages! Drawn cartoons even!* Why, that rotten, no-good...

I turned the pages, reading what Travis had scribbled on each one.

Then—a whistle. Agent Fury!

No! He couldn't be back yet!

I checked my phone. It was 5:05. I must have lost track of time. So now I had to fly—this was real live breaking and entering. Okay, not breaking, but definitely entering.

I tore down the stairs and pushed the cat door open with my foot. I shoved the binder through the opening, then got down on my belly to shimmy through.

My head—through.

My shoulders—through.

My hips—

Crappity Crap Crap! STUCK!

"Opal!" I called out in a stage whisper.

And then she was there, eyeball to eyeball with me, yanking on my arms, pulling so hard I thought my shoulders would be ripped right from their sockets.

But then, POP! My hips cleared the door and I was out, lying in the flower bed and panting hard, Opal lying half across me and breathing hard too.

"Come on, let's go!" I whispered. And again, the reverb through our phones screamed.

"Shut that off!" My words echoed over and over again, bouncing back and forth from one phone to the other.

I breathed a sigh of relief as Opal clambered off me and got to her feet. I pushed myself up onto my hands and knees and was ready to sprint away when a sharp blow between my shoulder blades knocked me flat.

"Fancy meeting you here, *Dirk*."

I got to my feet and dusted my clothes off.

"We were just leaving," I said. "Now get out of my way."

"Not so fast," Travis said. "I think my mom would like to hear about how you've been sneaking into our house when we're gone."

"You have no proof," Opal said.

"You're in my backyard. And you've got stuff from my room in your hands."

She clutched my binder even tighter to her chest. "This isn't yours and you know it."

I held up my hand to get Opal to stop. "You tell your mom I went into your house, and I tell her you've been selling tests."

Lucinda came running into the yard, breathless. "Oh no! I tried to stop him, guys, really I did."

Travis gave Lucinda a derisive look. "I can't believe you. So desperate you'd even bring Loser Lu in on your little games."

I glared at him. "Just shut your fat mouth, Travis! There's nothing wrong with Lucinda. It's you that's the loser."

"Thanks, Darren," Lucinda said. "I agree totally. Now that I know what you're really like, Travis. You...you..."

She kicked him then. Hard. In the shin.

I couldn't believe it. Lucinda had actually *kicked* Travis!

Travis was hopping on one foot, clutching his other leg. Opal started to snicker. And then she was laughing out loud. The sound was so cheerful, so musical, so *catching*, that I started laughing too. And then Lu said, "Take that. And if you do one more thing to hurt one more person, I will make sure you hurt a lot worse than that."

"Okay! Okay!" Travis said, still hopping. "I never meant…"

"Never meant what?"

"To hurt anybody," Travis said miserably.

"Yeah right," Opal said. "You probably never meant to steal tests either. Or humiliate Darren. Or pick on Lu. You just had a big oops."

"Kind of. Yeah," he said.

His eyes met mine. I got a glimpse of the old Travis in there. Or at least I thought I did.

"Spill it," I said.

His whole body seemed to droop all at once.

He nodded toward the door—the real one. "Come in, then."

"Yeah. Sure," Opal said. "Two seconds ago you were, like, 'I'm going to mess you up for breaking into my house.' And now we're going to sit down and have milk and cookies with you? Get real. Come on, Darren, Lu. Let's go."

My eyes held Travis's. "You guys go on without me. Travis and I have some stuff to talk about."

Lucinda's mouth dropped open. "You can't!"

I glanced over at Opal, and she shrugged her shoulders.

"Yeah. He can, Lu. And maybe he should. Let's go." She turned to me again and said, "We got your back, okay, Darren?"

"I know," I said.

Opal got up on her tiptoes, my notebook still in hand, and kissed my cheek. Then she and Lu took off.

I followed Travis around to the side door and into the house. I sat down at the kitchen table while he poured two glasses of milk. He got the box of Oreos out and passed me a stack.

"So, you know how Conner is about his stuff," he started.

I knew. His older brother, Conner, was a beast about not letting Travis touch anything that was his. He practically made Travis sign disclaimers before breathing.

"Well, I busted his iPad."

I whistled, long and low. "Those are really expensive, aren't they?"

"A fortune. And I have to pay him every single penny back. By Christmas."

"Where you gonna get the mon—"

I stopped and stared at him.

Duh.

"So that's why you sold the tests."

"Yeah." He couldn't look at me—*wouldn't* look at me—as he talked. "Conner suggested it. Said it was a quick way to make a buck. I didn't have any better ideas."

"You could have said no."

"I could have. But I didn't."

"You could have asked me for help! I would have loaned you some cash!"

He coughed. "Like you have any? Come on, dude. What would you do, start up a bake sale for me? I thought it would be easy. But I only had a few buyers."

"Waldo..." I said.

"And the guys from the Detention Gang."

My eyes snapped from my Oreos to his face.

"But once they bought the tests, they owned me too. Waldo? He didn't do anything. But the other guys... Well, turns out they didn't *use* the tests. So I had no insurance. Nothing I could hold over them. But since they bought them from me..."

"They owned you."

"Yeah."

"And the next thing you knew, they had you doing their dirty work. Like shaking down kids on the buses for lunch money," I said, connecting the dots.

"Uh-huh. They oh so generously let me keep a percentage of the take. To pay down my debt to Conner."

"I can't believe you didn't tell me."

He snorted. "Yeah right—you're agent Dirk Daring, a force for good in the world. A regular Bruce Wayne. I knew you'd get all sniffy at me."

I crossed my arms. "Well, you're right. I would have. I would have told you not to do it."

Travis laughed, a sharp, dark laugh.

"Maybe yes, maybe no. Turns out you're not so squeaky clean after all. Are you? You were pretty quick to throw me to the wolves when Waldo threatened you."

"That's not the same thing at all!" I cried.

"Oh, isn't it?"

I sat there, staring at my cookie tower.

"Why didn't you tell me where you were really going every Tuesday? Why did you have to make up that karate story?"

He swallowed. Hard.

"I was...oh come on, Darren! You're already so much smarter than me! I couldn't stand you knowing I was...you know."

"I am NOT smarter than you!" I yelled at him. "It's you that always has the good ideas. It's you that always figures out how to do stuff! It's you that knows what's cool and what's dorky and keeps me from making a fool of myself. It's you who had everything! It's you who was, like, my—"

I gulped, leaving the end of that sentence unsaid.

Travis was shaking his head. Shaking it, and shaking it, and shaking it.

"And you showed everyone my journal. Why'd you do that?"

Travis squirmed. "Jeez...I don't know. You were always going on about it. And it was just sitting in my backpack. I could feel the dumb thing pressing into my back and...I dunno. I just did."

"You just did. Real nice. Brill."

"I know," Travis said. "I know."

I shook my head. "These last few days...they've been, like...the worst days of—"

He got up from the table.

"Look, I'm sorry. Okay? Really. I don't blame you if you never want to speak to me again. Amber and I shouldn't have done what we did. I was just so damn mad at you for turning on me like that."

I took a deep, ragged breath.

"I'm sorry too. I should never have done what I did either. It was wrong."

"Do you think we can be friends again?"

"I don't know," I said, my eyes sliding back to my stack of Oreos. "We'll have to see." I pushed my chair back. "Look, I gotta go. Lu and Opal will be waiting for me."

Travis put his hand on my arm. "You know there's still one more mission to go, Dirk. Practically begging for you to do it."

I stopped in my tracks. Travis's fingers tightened on my bicep.

"You know it in your gut, Darren. It's the right thing to do. Your toughest mission yet. And the most important."

He was right. There *was* one more mission. It demanded completion.

"Let me quarterback it. For you," Travis said. "Please."

Our eyes met. A long, debt-tallying, promise-making eye meet.

"I'll think about it," I said.

The Final Mission.
jg76LKJvx3256BC3 De-encrypted.
Go Fish.

Travis's voice buzzed in my ear. "Team 1?"

I glanced over at Agent Jewel. Shot her a questioning eyebrow. She gave me a curt nod.

"We're a go."

My ear buzzed again.

"Team 2?"

I heard a giggle, also in my ear. "We're good too."

"Team 3?"

"Can you just call me Amber, Trav? It's kind of stupid for you to call me a team when I'm alo—"

"Roger that, Amber. Sounds like you're all set too. Now pay attention, teams. Because action begins in…3…2…1…go!"

On cue, Agent Jewel and I entered the schoolyard.

"So it was the most awesome birthday ever!" she said, her voice pitched loud and high. "I got this new purse—you like it, D? It's a Miss Sixty! And I got cash—oodles of it—from my gramma Sal and my aunt Jo. She's the rich one." She smiled broadly, waving her purse exaggeratedly in my general direction. "Goin' to the mall right after school to spend it!"

As Agent Jewel kept running out her line, I scanned our surroundings. Left, right, left, right, I checked for our prey.

Yes, there they were, two of the goons from the Detention Gang. Snouts snuffling the air.

"I saw these awesome bright red boots last week. They cost, like, $300, but I can buy 'em now! Woo-hoo! My aunt was, like, soooo generous!"

The enemy smelled our lure. They were drawn to us like speckled trout to a tied fly.

"First nibble," I whispered into the mic clipped inside my jacket collar.

"Roger that," Travis said.

From the corner of my eye, I spotted Team 2, Agent Fury and Agent Waldo, hard at work. Simulating a romantic conversation on the swings. I noted the excellent prep work: Fury's backpack was flung carelessly on the ground, her Hello Kitty wallet poking out the top. Greenbacks flashing like spinning spoons.

And sure enough, there were Lorne and Micah, Detention Specialists, swimming closer to the irresistible lure...

"Looks like Team 2 has got something on the line too," I said into my jacket.

"Good. What about Amber? Do you see her?"

"Negative."

"Amber?" I heard Travis say. "You okay?"

No answer.

My gut tightened.

We had to get this right. Everything depended on it. If our mission failed, we'd be swimming with the fishes.

"So what do you think, Darren? If you had a few hundred bucks to spend, would you buy a netbook or an iPad?" Opal rambled on.

And then they were on us. Circling like sharks.

"Morning, Opal. Morning, Dirk," Crandall Higgins sniggered.

"Happy birthday, Opal," Tom Chee said with a sneer.

"How old are you now? Like, 10?" Crandall said, giving her shoulder a shove.

"Hey! Leave her alone, Crandall!" I said loudly.

They both laughed. "Whatcha going to do to us, spyboy? Vaporize us with your stun gun?" They laughed again.

"Get lost," Opal said, clutching her purse to her chest.

"Why should we?"

"Yeah? Who's gonna make us? Sounds like you had a big payday," Tom said, reaching for the purse.

"Get your hands off me!" Opal yelled. "Don't touch my purse!"

The next thing I knew, Crandall had me in a head-lock, and Tom had pushed Opal to the ground. He was ripping open her purse and rifling through it.

"Where's the cash, kid?" he said with a snarl.

"Can you say that a bit louder?" I said as politely as I could with my jaw pinioned between Crandall's forearm and bicep. "They can't hear you in the bleachers."

Both goons followed my gaze. About half the student body was sitting in the stands. They had been quietly filing out through the gym doors. Under the direction—no, command—of Agent Amber.

"What the—!" Tom said.

What the what the what the! The echoing words rang out from the PA system, filling the schoolyard with the humiliating sound of a bully bleating.

Didn't I tell you Travis was a genius? At the crack of dawn, he had come down to the field and hooked up the PA speakers to his computer. Don't ask me how.

Tom's eyes went wide. Crandall gulped.

"Holy crap (*crapcrapcrap*)! What did you freaks do (*doodoodoodoodoo*)?" Their words were amplified a thousandfold by the loudspeakers. The bleachers roared with laughter.

Opal grabbed her purse back from Tom. "We 'freaks' decided it was time to shine some light on your secrets (*retsretsretsrets*). And end your reign of terror (*rorororor*). Once and for all (*allallall*)."

I threw one hand up in the air and spun my wrist three times. The signal for our B teams to advance.

Vero, Louie and Henry came trotting over. Did I mention they had just made the football team?

Together, the five of us made a human net around Tom and Crandall. We escorted our catch to the football field—50-yard line.

At the same time, Waldo and Lucinda, with a little help from their own backup team, had gotten a hold of Lorne and Micah. They carried them by the wrists and ankles over to us. Dropped them at our feet with an audible thump (*umpump*).

"That's it, guys (*guysguysguys*). No more shakedowns (*downsdownsdowns*). You're finished (*ishedishedished*)," Opal said, wiping her hands.

Another roar rose from the crowd.

Waldo pumped his fist in the air. "Come on, Preston (*tontonton*)! Let's hear it (*ritritrit*)! No more shakedowns! No more shakedowns! No more shakedowns!"

The kids in the stands took up the chant. "No more shakedowns! No more shakedowns! No more shakedowns!"

The combined roar from the kids and loudspeakers was deafening. And might I add fantastic? Abso-freaking-lutely fantastic.

I drew my hand across my throat—my signal to T-Bone to cut the loudspeaker connection. He gave me a thumbs-up from the top bleacher, then started making his way down the stairs. He belonged with the rest of us now, at our moment of glory.

"We got you guys red-handed," I told our netted fish. "We got eyewitnesses." I pointed to the stands. "Audio recordings. And video too." I showed them the mic, and the camera, disguised as a button on my sweater. "Your jig is up."

"Don't think you're going to get away with this," Crandall said, struggling to his feet. A smashed tuna sandwich, thrown by someone in the stands, was stuck in his hair. "There are lots of dark alleys in this town, kiddies."

"Dark alleys don't scare me," I said with a wink at Opal. "I'm Dirk Daring, Secret Agent."

"Me neither," she said. "I'm Allegra Montefiore. Alleys are my specialty."

"I'm Agent Fury," said Lucinda, giggling.

"So we're doing introductions, then? You fellas already know me. I'm Waldo. Agent-in-arms AND school president."

Travis came running up, breathing hard. "Agent T-Bone reporting. What did I miss?"

"Nothing. Just these losers wetting themselves," Waldo said. "Nice work on the PA system, by the way." He gave Travis a fist bump.

A sudden murmur swept through the crowd.

I looked left, right. There, coming from the gym doors, was Amber. And Bonaparte. They marched over, flanked by two security guards.

"Here you go," Amber said. "Those are the true troublemakers at Preston Middle School. The ringleaders of the so-called Detention Gang."

Bonaparte's seagull eyes grew even beadier, if possible, more seagull-y, than normal. "Crandall. Micah." He spat out their names. "I should have known you'd be involved in something like this."

"I tried to tell you," Travis said. "But nooooo, you said I was making it up to try and save my own skin. Well, now you'll have to believe me. We got them in the act. On tape."

"And now you'll have to do something about it," Amber said.

Waldo stepped forward. "Our school code says there will be zero tolerance given to any student involved in a criminal act on school property. And theft is a criminal act…so you'll have to expel them."

Bonaparte shot him a beady glare. "You can rest assured we will follow all appropriate procedures. Now get to class, children. The bell is about to ring."

Bonaparte nodded to the security guards to haul the Detention Gang away. Then he turned on his heel and marched back to the double doors.

Meanwhile, kids streamed down from the bleachers, surrounding us in a sea of high fives.

I stood there, a big idiot grin on my face. I looked left, right, left, right, from the face of one friend to another.

Opal, Lucinda.

Travis. Amber.

Even ~~Wal-~~. Even Jason.

Who'da thunk it? Our little band of misfits, it turned out, made a pretty good team.

The activation email arrived on April Fools' Day. I knew, however, it was no joke.

It read, Bo Diddley. 4/2. 16:00:00.

Even as I read the words, the message disappeared.

Poof.

Gone from my screen. Inbox. Hard drive.

As always.

At the designated time and place, I ordered my usual meal—a cheeseburger and fries. No pickle. No onion.

I picked up the burger gingerly. Bit into it gently. Chewed slowly, looking left, right, left, right. No one was watching.

SNZZT! My teeth chomped on something hard. Metallic.

I lifted my napkin to my mouth. Spit the object into it surreptitiously.

It was a phone memory card.

I made no sudden moves. I simply finished my burger. Paid my bill. Sauntered from the Diddley, the memory card concealed within my palm. Sat on a park bench and slipped it into my phone. Turned it back on.

A text message appeared on my phone's screen.

Messages	**redpuppy**

> Look to your right. In the garbage can, wrapped in a ketchup-stained piece of tissue, you will find a lime-green retainer case. Retrieve it. Tomorrow at 19:00:00, a car (you will find the jpg showing the car and license plate number on your phone's picture list, DSC1505) transporting the ambassador from Kanakistan will travel down Main Street and park in front of the Capitol Theater (DSC1506).

HE IS AN ENEMY AGENT. Your mission will be to attach the GPS device (the retainer), by its embedded magnets, to the undercarriage of the car.

Now look to your right. You should see a soccer ball sitting under the Norway maple. That is both an aid to your cover and your comm device— a microphone is embedded in the airhole. Obtain the ball immediately after you have retrieved the retainer case. You can report on the success of your mission by speaking directly into the ball.

When your mission is complete, you can dispose of the ball in the used-clothing donation box on the corner of Main and Wesleyan (DSC1507). Your counterpart from HQ will retrieve it.

As usual, destroy this memory card once you have committed the instructions herein to memory.

> We wish you best of luck in your mission, and trust you will achieve your usual high level of success.

I turned off the phone. Removed the memory card and put it in my mouth. I bit down on it, and bit again, until the card was nothing but broken black and coppery grit. I spit the debris into the garbage pail as I reached for the retainer case. Wiped the remainder off my tongue as I kicked the ball high into the air. Caught it, on its return to earth, in my arms.

Tomorrow I'd be running down Main Street, dribbling my soccer ball. When—oops! I'd "lose control" of it, and it would roll under a car parked in front of the theater. I'd get down on my hands and knees to retrieve it, simultaneously affixing the GPS device to the undercarriage.

No one would suspect that the unassuming boy with the errant soccer ball was Dirk Daring, Secret Agent. None would suspect the car had been compromised, and the enemy agent who used it would now be in full sight of The Agency.

Because sometimes the most difficult missions are literally child's play. And who better to engage in such play than a child?

NEWPORT GAZETTE

APRIL 3

Newport enjoyed the arrival of a host of dignitaries and celebrities at the opening of the Newport Film Festival, the premiere event of the Newport Film Society. Among the attendees were Izaak Renyshyn, the newly appointed ambassador for the Republic of K...

ACKNOWLEDGMENTS

I would like to gratefully acknowledge financial support from the Ontario Arts Council Writer's Reserve program.

Helaine Becker is the bestselling author of more than fifty books for children and young adults, including the "enduring Canadian Christmas classic" *A Porcupine in a Pine Tree* and the giggle-inducing *Ode to Underwear*. She's also a three-time winner of the Silver Birch Award and a two-time winner of the Lane Anderson Award for Science Writing for Children. Helaine lives in Toronto with her husband and her dog, Ella. For more information, visit www.helainebecker.com.